'Is that why you're refusing to talk? Are you angry with me because you thought I'd forgotten you? I should be the angry one. I didn't know how to contact you, but, as you said downstairs, I'm famous . . . why didn't *you* find *me*? Or was getting engaged to my brother just a clever ploy to get to me?'

'I got engaged to your brother because I happen to be in love with him,' said Helen fiercely, recoiling from his tender amusement. 'Look, Alexander, you're obviously tired after your flight. Why don't you go and lie down——'

'Don't patronise me, Helen.'

'I'm not patronising you, but you're obviously disturbed——'

'You always did have that effect on me.'

'There you go again . . . talking as if we knew each other. We don't. I've never seen you before today.'

'And that's the way you're determined to play it?' he said.

'I'm not playing, Alex. I genuinely have no idea what you're talking about,' she said helplessly.

'Am I just a face in the crowd, now?' he sneered. His laugh was harsh with disgust, for her or himself, or perhaps for both of them. 'I thought a woman never forgot her first lover.'

ANOTHER TIME

BY

SUSAN NAPIER

MILLS & BOON LIMITED
ETON HOUSE   18-24 PARADISE ROAD
RICHMOND   SURREY   TW9 1SR

*First published in Great Britain 1989
by Mills & Boon Limited*

© Susan Napier & Aspasia Trust 1989

*Australian copyright 1989
Philippine copyright 1989
This edition 1989*

ISBN 0 263 76285 8

*Set in Times Roman 10 on 11 pt.
01-8904-60523 C*

Made and printed in Great Britain

PROLOGUE

IT was her.

Alexander Knight stared at the photograph, the letter which had accompanied it crumpling in the involuntary fist of his left hand. Forgotten was the filthy Manhattan weather he had been fluently cursing when he had stormed into his ground-floor apartment, forgotten was the frustration he had just endured at the hands of an ill-informed television host, forgotten was the formal dinner he was already running late for, and the beautiful woman whom he had arranged to escort.

It was her.

He had waited for so long for this moment and yet, now that it was upon him, his paramount feeling was one of betrayal. It was unreasonable and unwarranted, but then, human emotions rarely conformed to impartial notions of justice.

Anger and bitterness at the irony of the situation drove him into his gleaming stainless-steel kitchen where he flicked on the coffee-maker as he shrugged out of his wet overcoat, not taking his eyes off the photograph he had propped against the sleek black telephone. Five years ago he would have headed for the Scotch bottle rather than the coffee-maker. Five years ago he would have handled his feelings by going out and getting drunk and maybe smashing up a few things while he reviled his accursed fate. Maybe he would have taken a woman to ease the loneliness, and ended up even lonelier than ever. Thanks to the woman in the photograph, the laughing woman wrapped in another man's arms, he was no longer prey to such self-destructive impulses. He had learned to channel his negative emotions into positive thoughts and actions, and he did so now, automatically, as he stroked a long, supple thumb over the woman's face in the glossy photograph. Even touching her by proxy stirred him. Oh, yes, it was her all right. Her hair was a different colour and she was no longer as slender and fragile, but her eyes were the same... an indescribable shade of green, filled with the joy of life. She didn't look any older than she had five years ago, but then, angels didn't fade, they merely became brighter and more beautiful with the passage of time.

Angel in the Dark. That was how she had appeared to him. And while she was with him the oppressive darkness had lifted and he had seen a way out. Her warmth had healed some deep, cold wound in him, her innocence and passion had reawakened him to the inherent sweetness of life.

Hong Kong had only been meant as a brief stopover, on the way to another war which would enhance his reputation as a journalist and spawn another of his formula best-sellers.

He had awoken the afternoon following his arrival, his head pounding from the amount of booze he had consumed on the interconnecting flights from South America, not even knowing what country he was in, only grateful for the absence of gunfire outside his window.

He had gone to the party that night out of desperation, to still the ceaseless voices inside his head that chattered to him in the dark. Wherever he went there were always invitations to be had, his reputation saw to that. His vices were many, acquired over the years like an armoured skin to hide his vulnerability from others, and from himself. He smoked, he drank, he mingled sociably with the merchants of death from every side, he used sex as a physical release in much the same way that his slick novels were a mental one.

What had made *her* so different? Initially he had noticed her because of her solitude, even in the midst of the crowd. Alone but not lonely. He had felt envy, resentment, desire. She had looked so small and fragile, her faintly oriental looks clashing with the ridiculous falsity of that white-blonde hair, but he had instinctively sensed an inner resilience, a waiting, listening, unshockable vitality that had made him want to go over and pour out his black soul.

Her sweet serenity had not recoiled from his sullen assault, and against all odds he had found his absolution. Purists might call what went on between two strangers in an anonymous hotel room by a harsher name, but Alex knew the arid alternatives all too well, and what he and his nameless angel had done that night was to make love, in the literal sense... creating it out of the nothingness that had existed before.

Afterwards he had seen the world through different eyes. She had gone, but she had left behind the gift of her grace. He had gone back to his wars, but now he was no longer haunted by dark pessimism, now he wrote with love and compassion instead of cynicism and contempt. The reformation had not been easy, but his inspiration had never faltered. And always he remembered... hoped...

For five years he had been more than half in love with a beautiful, romantic illusion, and now that illusion was within reach. Now he knew her name and where to find her. Now he must decide if she wanted to be found, and if he was willing to face the inevitable consequences of finding her.

He smiled, mind and body tautening at the challenge.

Alexander Knight was not a *completely* reformed man.

CHAPTER ONE

'Ouch!' The bride jumped.

'Sorry, Helen.' Hannah's voice was filtered through a mouthful of pins as she readjusted a seamline. She sat back on her heels and sighed, spitting the pins into her hand. 'I just can't get that proportion right. I have the terrible feeling that I made some elementary error in the drafting, and now it's returning to haunt me.'

Helen Smith grinned down at her prospective mother-in-law's harassed face. Hannah was a magnificent dressmaker, but was never satisfied with the results even when, to everyone else, they looked perfect.

'It's gorgeous, Hannah,' she said soothingly. 'The fit feels just right and it looks great...or it will when it's all sewn up.' At the moment the heavy cream silk was a mass of pins and tacking, but even Helen, no dressmaker herself, could see the makings of something spectacular.

Hannah sighed again. 'I guess I'm just having second thoughts about the design. Wedding dresses are usually thought of in terms of lace and frills and veils.'

Helen laughed. 'This was *your* idea to begin with, Hannah. *You're* the one who encouraged me to think unique! It's a bit late in the day to get cold feet. I thought that the practice dress was a dream...perhaps I should just wear that.'

Hannah smiled reluctantly, tucking a strand of faded blonde hair into the thick bun at the nape of her neck. 'And the bride wore calico? I'd never live it down.' She stood up with remarkable agility for a woman in her early sixties, and backed away, crossing her arms over her plump breasts as she regarded her efforts with a critical stare. 'It'll certainly make Ida sit up and take notice, won't it?'

'Definitely.' Ida was Hannah's sister, and just as skilful with a needle. She had married her own daughter off three months before in a dress which the portraits showed was splendidly traditional. Their rivalry was amicably intense and one of the reasons, Helen had been amused to realise, that Hannah had been so eager to shake off tradition and go for something dramatic and unusual.

Hannah had found her inspiration in an exhibition of Japanese ceremonial robes at the Auckland Art Gallery. She had taken photographs and excitedly shown them to Helen.

'Why not capitalise on your heritage?' Hannah had said. 'Something like this kimono over a slimline under-dress would look beautiful, and Mrs Harrison could do the dragon embroidery and use pearls and paua shell for the scales.'

'My great-grandmother was Chinese, not Japanese,' Helen had pointed out mildly, taken instantly by the idea herself. At five-foot-four, with glossy, jet-black hair cut in a collar-length bob to add volume to its silky straightness, and almond-shaped grey-green eyes set above high, flat cheekbones in an oval ivory-skinned face, she knew that she didn't look like the average New Zealand woman. So Hannah had gone to work on the photographs and come up with a long-sleeved, figure-hugging underdress in thin silk with a stiff, wrapover outer robe with flared sleeves and a wide, embroidered waistband. The dragon embroidery across her shoulder-blades had been carefully copied from a book of orien-tal art, and was repeated around the flared hem of the robe which dipped to sweep the floor behind her. The heavy silk of the robe had been hideously expensive, but Helen had been quite happy to pay since Greg's parents, with typical open-handed generosity, had insisted on paying for the rest of the wedding. Helen's own parents were dead and her elder sister, Susan, lived abroad with her husband and three pre-schoolers, and couldn't spare the time to come over and help with arrangements before the wedding, so Helen had been extremely grateful for the support, financial and moral, of her 'second' family.

'I'm not going to hide this away in the back of a wardrobe after the wedding, you know, Hannah,' said Helen firmly. 'The underdress will make a lovely formal gown, and I'm going to use the coat as an embroidered wall display—you know, like those kimonos that were framed at the exhibition.'

'What a lovely idea!' Hannah flushed with pleasure and Helen felt a shared warmth. Greg's family had made her feel totally welcome from the very first time they had met. 'Perhaps you could hang it on that big wall in Greg's lounge,' she added slyly, 'instead of the modern monstrosity he has there now.'

'Greg says that monstrosity is worth a lot of money,' said Helen, who privately shared her opinion.

Hannah sniffed in maternal disgust. 'Thank goodness he has no say in your wedding dress is all *I* can say. I don't think that boy has much taste of his own...or why did he let that decorator loose in his home? I would never let anyone else decide what I should live with!'

Helen grinned. 'That boy' was thirty, six years older than Helen, a cultured man who had travelled a great deal on business. He owned his own import/export business, and the only reason he had got a decorator in was that he had been too busy to do it himself and didn't trust his mother's comfortably middle-class tastes!

It was a business trip that had brought them together in the first place. They had met on a flight from Sydney to Auckland. Greg had been coming back from a trade fair in Japan, and Helen had been on the last leg of a journey that had taken two years. She had been on a shoe-string tour of Europe with some friends, paying her way with her talents as a hand-knitter, making and selling her unique sweaters wherever she went.

She had already been planning another trip when she'd met Greg, and looked forward to accompanying him on his business trips. He had helped bring her more orders for her work than she had ever had at one time before, and the pressure was such that she might have to give up the stall she shared at Victoria Park Market in central Auckland with two other knitters. However, she liked dealing with the public and thrived on seeing people admiring her work, whether they bought or not, and didn't want to turn her craft into the kind of regimented business that Greg had suggested was more efficient.

'I'm so glad that Greg's marrying you,' said Hannah suddenly as she gathered up the sewing debris from the carpet of the small, sunny room of the big, old house that she used for her dress-making. 'He's been happier these last few months than he's been for years. I was afraid at one time that he might not ever marry——' Hannah stopped, looking uncomfortable.

'It's all right, Hannah,' said Helen. 'Greg told me that he was in love once before and that it was pretty serious. I know all about the family trauma it caused and we agreed that it was in the past. I'm only sorry that he was hurt...'

'We all were, in one way or another, but it was worse for the two boys. Up until then we were such a close family, even though there was a certain amount of rivalry between them, that sort of thing is natural between siblings who are close in age. Still, as you say, it's spilt milk now...'

And the family was still estranged. Helen knew that Greg had been both relieved and disturbed when the wedding acceptance had arrived with its foreign stamp. He had always felt over-shadowed by his elder brother, who had been so proficient at everything, so talented and so at ease with his popularity, but he had not de-

liberately set out to break up his engagement. He had
fallen in love with his brother's fiancée and she with
him, in spite of their best efforts to fight the mutual
attraction. They had been found out and there had been
a bitter, black row with wild accusations flying thick and
fast. In the end, neither brother had won, for the girl
had run away from the ugly situation...and here Helen
could detect in Greg's voice the echoes of an old pain
that still had the power to hurt.

Hannah cocked her head at the sound of her husband
answering the doorbell. 'Who's that Nick's talking to,
I wonder? Surely he's not inviting anyone in so close to
dinner? You know, you don't have to rush off afterwards, Helen. You're welcome to stay the night in the
spare room if there's no one at home...'

'OK, thanks,' said Helen, who hadn't looked forward
to returning to an empty flat. She shared with two other
girls...one of whom was an agency nurse working mainly
night-shifts, and the other a nanny, with the appropriate
name of Serena, who was currently employed in a live-
in job with a visiting diplomat and his family. 'Greg said
he was going to phone tonight, but if he doesn't get any
answer at the flat he'll probably know to ring here.'
Whenever Greg went away on one of his buying or selling
trips—and over half of his time was spent travelling—
he always rang her every two days, uncaring of the incredible expenses he ran up on their invariably long and
affectionate chats. Once, when she had remonstrated,
he had laughed. 'I always bring one of your samples,
don't I? That makes all this sweet-talk tax-
deductible...not to mention giving me something of
yours to cuddle during the long, lonely nights!'

'Next time I'll knit you a teddy bear instead of a
jumper,' she had teased.

The visitor's voice, now in the hallway, sounded oddly
familiar, and Hannah squeaked. 'My goodness, that
sounds like Greg, but it can't be, can it? He's not due

back until Monday. It certainly *sounds* like him.' Quickly she whisked off the wide waistband and began un-pinning the front of the undergown, which would have tiny pearl buttons all the way from the little stand-up collar to hem. 'Surely Nick wouldn't be so silly as to bring him along here? He knows very well what we're working on . . . but you'd better nip upstairs and change. I know Greg won't be able to stay away once he knows you're here——'

Helen clutched at the gaping front of the gown as Hannah's husband, a spritely old man who was revel-ling in his retirement, appeared in the doorway.

'Sorry, girls,' he said, his brown eyes dark with a re-pressed excitement. 'But we have a guest and I didn't think you'd want to stand on ceremony when you knew who it was . . .'

'Alex!' After a startled instant Hannah flew across the room like a young girl and threw herself into the arms of the tall, denim-clad man who had appeared beside her husband in the doorway.

'Hello, Mum.' Alexander Knight took the impact of her love easily with his big body, grinning casually as if it had been a week rather than a year since his last visit home.

'Alex.' His mother was laughing and nearly crying at the same time. 'Oh, Alex, we didn't expect you for *weeks*, what are you doing here *now*?'

'I was able to re-arrange the publicity schedule for the book so that I could come early and stay longer.'

'Oh, Alex, that's wonderful . . . but why didn't you warn us? I haven't got your room ready yet.'

'I wanted it to be a surprise.' This time his smile and voice were gentle, and Helen, watching from the side-lines, felt an odd pang. At that moment the man's eyes lifted from his mother's excited face and meshed with hers.

His eyes were dark and penetrating, almost black, and the politely warm smile Helen had been preparing to don froze on her lips. Then the fleeting tension disappeared as she realised the reason for it. He was so very like Greg. His eyes were a shade darker, perhaps, and so was his skin, but his hair was the same dark gold, though worn inelegantly shaggy instead of neatly cut. His face was the same shape as Greg's, too, handsomely proportioned, the broad cheekbones balanced by the firm sweep of his jaw. The most striking difference between the brothers was that Alexander Knight's vast experience of life had obviously hardened him: the dark eyes were hooded, almost secretive, as if possessed of a dangerous knowledge that he was daring the world to guess at. The lines at the corner of those knowing eyes hadn't been etched there by laughter, and yet Helen sensed a great capacity for humour, an appetite for life that didn't appear blunted by years of highly publicised self-indulgence.

'Alex?' His attention was drawn by his mother, but he didn't take his eyes off Helen and she could feel herself begin to blush at his overt interest. 'I said, how long can you stay?'

'As long as it takes,' he murmured obliquely. His gaze fell to where Helen was trying to keep the unfinished gown from gaping open. His mouth curved. 'Hello,' he said softly, and watched her blush heighten at the teasing, sexy intonation.

'Oh, goodness!' Hannah turned back, slightly flustered. 'I forgot to introduce you, didn't I? Come and meet Helen, but you mustn't say anything about the dress to Greg.' She tugged her son over to where Helen stood.

'This, as you must have guessed, is our famous son, Alex. Alex, this is Helen Smith.'

'Smith? That really *is* your name?' Helen felt a ripple of annoyance at his amusement. Did he think she was masquerading under an alias?

'Yes.' She held out her hand formally. 'I'm pleased to meet you, Mr Knight. I've never met anyone famous before.'

His hand, holding hers, tightened fractionally, his eyes narrowing. 'Except me, Helen.' He gave her Christian name quiet emphasis.

Helen withdrew her hand with difficulty, confused. 'I . . . yes, but we've never met before.'

'Haven't we?' The query was mild, but the steady boldness of his gaze made her feel uneasy.

'No.'

'You seem very certain.'

'I am.' She was beginning to feel annoyed by his silly game-playing. Even his parents were regarding them oddly. Was this his idea of being pleasant to his brother's fiancée? Did he automatically play verbal games with every woman he met? Perhaps he expected her to fall all over him because he was a famous author. 'I'm sure I would have remembered,' she said firmly.

His mother intervened. 'You're probably just re-calling her face from the photo I sent you. Have you just flown in, Alex? Did you bring his cases in, Nicholas?'

'They're still at the hotel.' At last Alex removed his disturbing gaze from Helen's flushed face.

'Hotel?' Hannah looked shocked, and Nicholas frowned.

'The publisher does all the bookings, I just turn up on time to catch my flights,' said Alex soothingly. 'I managed to evade the welcoming committee at the airport, but my luggage didn't. It's gone on to the Regent. Besides, I didn't know whether you already had visitors . . .' He spread his hands. His fingers looked strong and supple, probably from all that exercise on the type-writer . . . capable, creative hands, Helen found herself thinking irrelevantly.

'Only Helen, and you know there's always room for you, Alex,' his mother chided him.

Something quickened in Alex's eyes as he looked at Helen. 'You're living here?'

'Just staying the night,' she said, wishing now that she could back out. 'But perhaps you'd prefer to have just family tonight, I——'

'Nonsense!' Hannah said firmly. 'You're already family, Helen, as far as we're concerned. A hotel, Alex, how could you think of such a thing?'

'I know the Regent's service isn't a patch on yours,' said Alex, straight-faced.

'Hmmm...don't imagine that just because we're glad to see you, you're going to be waited on hand and foot. All that hotel living you write home about is bound to spoil you. It'll do you good to live with ordinary folk for a while instead of jet-setting everywhere...'

'Yes, Mum.' Alex winked at his father, and for a moment Helen liked him. 'I suppose you're going to put a curfew on me, too?'

'From what I hear, my boy, you could do with one.' Hannah rose good-humouredly to the maternal bait. 'You've got horrible bags under your eyes and you're looking very tired and strained.'

'Jet lag,' said the big man meekly. 'I have another book preying on my mind and interfering with my sleep, and the publicity for the current one has become a real grind. I could do with some mother-smothering. Why don't I go back into town and pick up my bags and check out of the hotel? Then I can come back and you can stuff me with home-cooked goodies...'

'No, you stay here and talk to your mother, Alex.' His father patted him on the shoulder. 'You need to wind down. I've done nothing but potter in the garden all day. I'll go in and pick up your baggage, if you call and let them know. It's only a ten-minute drive at this time of the evening, and tea isn't ready yet.'

'Thanks, Dad. Here, take the car in the drive—it's rented—my publishers are picking up the tab for this visit, and since I'm saving them a hefty hotel bill...' Alex grinned as his father caught the keys tossed in his direction and saw what make the car was.

'I've always wanted to drive one of these...'

'I'll buy you one, if you like.'

Nicholas' rugged face creased. He was proud of his son's financial success, but not particularly impressed by it. 'Not *own* one, Alex, just drive one. Too many hassles in owning a beast like this. I won't be long, Hannah.'

'He'll be all right, Mum,' said Alex as his mother listened anxiously to the low, expensive growl of a car engine a minute or so later. 'You know he's always careful on the road.'

'Once a boy, always a boy,' said his mother. 'Your father was an awful tearaway when I first knew him.'

'And you've done a grand job of reformation.' His smile invited Helen to share the family joke, but although she smiled she still felt vaguely uneasy for no reason that she could name.

'Why don't you get yourself a drink while you're waiting, Alex? I must just go and see to dinner,' said his mother, her mind running ahead to ways to stretch the planned meal.

'Why don't I see to dinner, so you and Alex can talk?' offered Helen quickly.

'In your wedding dress?' murmured Alex, too close for comfort, his eyes telling her that he knew it was just an excuse to escape his unsettling company.

'Yes, run up and get back into your clothes, Helen, and then you two can get acquainted. Alex and I will have plenty of time to catch up if he's going to be staying here. Oh, and Alex, the telephone is in the hall now, not the kitchen. We had it moved when your father retired last year because he was always cluttering me up with his notes and calls, always when I needed the extra bench space . . .'

Her voice faded down the hall as Helen rustled towards the door. But Alex was there before her and he didn't stand aside.

'Well . . . Miss Smith,' said softly, in a mocking tone that she took instant exception to.

'Will you excuse me, please, Alex? I want to take off this dress.'

'My sentiments entirely.' His black eyes slid down to where her bare thigh was revealed by the parted folds of the skirt.

Perhaps it was the jet lag, thought Helen, struggling to give him the benefit of the doubt. She half smiled at him nervously, noticing that his pupils looked tiny in their dark chocolate surrounds. Maybe he was on drugs . . . cocaine or whatever was fashionable in the fast lane in which he lived.

'Excuse me,' she repeated more firmly.

'Running away, now that Hannah isn't here to protect you? You can't run far, Helen. We have to talk some time.'

To her relief he moved. 'I'm sure we will,' she said breathlessly as she brushed past and fled up the stairs. All the way up she felt his stare like a gun-sight trained on her back, and it was all she could do not to pick up her skirts and run.

In the safety of the spare bedroom she looked at herself in the full-length mirror, her heart still thumping erratically. It was so silly to let him upset her. She was a pretty girl and used to male attention. Usually she didn't mind flirting because it was all in fun, but underneath Alexander Knight's banter she had sensed a more serious purpose.

Helen slipped off the outer robe and carefully extricated herself from the tacked underdress. Clad in her lacy bra-slip and panties, she hung the gown against the door of the built-in wardrobe and turned to pick up her dress from the bed.

Alexander Knight was leaning against the closed bedroom door, his faded denim shirt pulling taut across his broad shoulders as he folded his arms over his chest.

'What do you think you're doing? This isn't your room!' Helen hissed furiously, snatching up her dress and holding it against her. Unfortunately it was a light cotton knit and there wasn't much of it.

'I know. Mine is along the hall,' he said, undisturbed by her outrage.

'Well, what are you doing in here, then?' she demanded. Her dress had no fastenings. To put it on she had to pull it over her head, and she could imagine the thrill *that* would give this impossible man—her slip was a mini one and if she lifted her arms he would get a front-seat view of the transparently frivolous bit of lace that masqueraded as intimate apparel.

'Didn't you expect me?' From the way he was studying her hemline, with a curve at the corner of that hard, sexy mouth, he was entirely cognisant of her dilemma. No doubt he knew women's underwear, and bodies, like the back of his hand . . . but not Helen's!

'What do you mean, *expect* you?' she snapped.

'Our little talk, remember?'

'I'm getting dressed,' she pointed out, through gritted teeth.

He shrugged. 'Don't mind me.'

'Oh, but I do mind,' she said furiously. 'I mind very much.' Not least because of the physical awareness he had managed to generate between them with a mere look. His gaze was faintly hungry, faintly humorous, faintly annoyed . . . as if *she* were the one playing teasing games. Greg never looked at her like that; his looks were always soft and warm and loving. 'How dare you invade my privacy——' she began breathlessly, determined to whip up her quite justifiable resentment, disgusted with herself for feeling a tiny bit *flattered* by that purely sexual appreciation.

'Come off it, Helen.' Alexander Knight shifted his shoulders impatiently against the solid wood of the door. In spite of their width and the solid hardness of his thighs revealed under the tightness of his denim jeans, Helen realised that the rest of him was quite lean and compact. It was his aura of self-command, his self-confidence that projected an impression of size, rather than his physical dimensions. 'We don't have an audience now. You don't have to pretend any more.'

'I don't know what you're talking about.'

His eyes narrowed. 'I can understand that you might find it embarrassing to acknowledge the truth in front of my mother and father, but I don't know what you expect to achieve by pretending with me. Or is it that you're afraid I'll tell Greg?'

'Tell Greg what?' She frowned at him suspiciously. 'Are you on some kind of drug?'

'I don't even use aspirin.'

'Maybe you had one too many drinks on the plane,' she persisted, wishing that he would move away from the door so that she could make a dash for the bathroom down the hall.

'Of fruit juice?' A dark blond eyebrow rose. 'I don't drink much either, these days. In fact, for the last few years I've lived an incredibly virtuous life.'

With those eyes? And that mouth and body? Helen scoffed. 'Even your own mother wouldn't believe *that*.'

'Is that why you're refusing to talk? Are you angry with me because you thought I'd forgotten you? I should be the angry one. I didn't know how to contact you, but, as you said downstairs, I'm famous...why didn't *you* find *me*? Or was getting engaged to my brother just a clever ploy to get to me?'

'I got engaged to your brother because I happen to be in love with him,' said Helen fiercely, recoiling from his tender amusement. 'I have no idea what the hell you're talking about. Now, will you please leave so that I can put my clothes on?'

'You know I can't do that. Not until we've settled this.'

'Settled *what*?' she cried in angry bewilderment.

'Us.'

'Us? There is no us. We've only just been introduced.' Suddenly uncaring of his all-knowing eyes, Helen turned her back and quickly pulled on her dress. It was scoop-necked with short sleeves, and covered her modestly to the knee, but when she turned again and saw Alexander's scorching look she might just as well have been naked.

'Stop looking at me like that,' she said, flushing wildly.

'I can't help it. You're even more beautiful than ever.'

'Look, Alexander, you're obviously tired after your flight. Why don't you go and lie down——'

'Don't patronise me, Helen.'

'I'm not patronising you, but you're obviously disturbed——'

'You always did have that effect on me.'

'There you go again...talking as if we know each other. We don't. I've never seen you before today...except on your book jackets.'

'And that's the way you're determined to play it?' he said, his dark eyes grim and determined.

'I'm not playing, Alex. I genuinely have no idea what you're talking about,' she said helplessly.

'Am I just a face in the crowd now?' he sneered. 'Have you had so many lovers since that you've forgotten who it was that initiated you into the delights of the flesh?' His laugh was harsh with disgust, for her or himself, or perhaps for both of them. 'I thought that a woman never forgot her first lover.'

Colour exploded into Helen's face. 'You *are* on drugs!' she accused. 'Either that or you're mad. We've never even *met*, let alone been lovers——'

'You're denying that you met me in Hong Kong five years ago? Oh, you were blonde then, both top and tail, but it looked too artificial against your skin to be your natural colouring.'

Helen's eyes blazed at his raw crudity. 'For your information,' she bit out, 'I have never dyed my hair in my life. I have never been anything but a natural brunette. And I have never been to Hong Kong in my life, let alone five years ago. In fact, I can prove it. I have a six-year-old passport. Do you want to see it?'

He didn't move, his eyes locked on hers as he probed the genuineness of her blistering triumph. She saw shock in the brown depths, and a bewilderment as intense as her own had been following his bizarre assault on her integrity. Her anger eased. It hadn't been a game to him, either; he had actually believed the nonsense he had spouted.

'Where were you, then, five years ago next month?' he asked finally in a voice totally devoid of emotion or aggression. Helen relaxed. She was getting through at last.

'I was in England,' she said gently. 'I went to England in the first week of October and stayed there for two months. Then I flew to the States, where my sister was living with her husband at the time. I lived with them for a year before I came back to New Zealand.'

'How old are you?'

'Twenty-four.'

'Nineteen...' he muttered. He shouldered himself away from the door and prowled towards her, but Helen no longer felt threatened, his expression of shock and regret was too real. 'Are you telling me the truth?'

'Of course I am . . . I told you, I can prove it with my visa stamps. Look, I don't know who your Helen Smith was, but it wasn't me.'

'I didn't know your—her—first name,' he said, coming to a frowning halt in front of her, hands thrust deep into his jeans pockets, staring intently at her, taking her features apart piece by piece and checking them against the vivid image in his memory. 'She told me her name was Smith, but I thought that was just a joke...'

'Maybe not. There are a hell of a lot of us Smiths in the world,' said Helen, trying not to flinch under that possessive stare.

'You look so very like her. I don't suppose you have a twin?' She shook her head. 'A double, then? My God, I was so sure...' He was talking almost to himself. He reached out and touched a finger to the creamy ivory of her cheek. She shifted uneasily.

'Five years is quite a long time. Maybe your memory is faulty.'

He dropped his hand, and this time his smile was without flirtatiousness. 'There's an old Spanish proverb: memory, like women, is usually unfaithful.'

'I'd take issue with half of that statement,' said Helen tartly, in defence of her sex.

'And I with the other half. I have a trained memory, it's been a godsend in my work.' The hooded eyes became unreadable. 'Are you faithful, then, Helen Smith?'

He meant to his brother. 'Yes.'

'Pity,' he murmured, every bit as sincere as she. 'You're so very like her.'

'Was she...special?' She was curious about the woman who had so obviously ensnared this sexual sophisticate.

'More than even I knew at the time.'

'Were you...in love with her?' As soon as she had asked, she knew that it was an absurd question. 'No, of course, you couldn't have been, you didn't even know her first name.'

'We never got around to exchanging polite pleasantries.'

Heat rose inside Helen as she realised what he meant. 'My God, you mean...you mean you only...it was only...'

'A one-night stand? Yes.' He found her shock amusing. 'But what a night!'

'And you thought that I was the kind of girl who...who...you thought that *I* went around having one-night stands with men I didn't know?' Helen's eyes were deep green with fury, and she was shaking with fresh outrage as she drew herself up to her full, generously curved five foot four. 'How dare you call me a tramp?'

'I wasn't aware I had. I can't speak for you, of course,' he said provokingly, fascinated by the hectic flush on the high cheekbones that made her almond eyes look faintly slanted, 'but *my* Miss Smith certainly wasn't a tramp. In fact, she was a virgin. In the morning when I woke to find her gone, the only sign that she had been there at all was her blood on the sheets. That, and her perfume on my skin and the taste of her still in my mouth, and my memory...'

'I don't want to hear this,' Helen choked, tingling all over at his pleasurable reminiscence. Did the man have no shame? Sex was an intimate, private thing between a man and a woman.

'She blushed, too. After we made love for the third time we took a bath together and she was pink all over. I got the impression that we could make love a thousand times and she would never loose that delightful combination of shyness and wonder that made her blush at her ability to arouse me...'

'Alex!' He seemed to have forgotten who he was talking to. He had that hungry expression again, and Helen could easily imagine him in a bathtub, broad shoulders slick and wet, cradling his woman between his legs as he—— 'Alex, stop it!'

'What? Oh...' The heat-glaze shimmered for a moment longer in his dark eyes before it faded. 'Sorry, Helen...but you're her double, I'm afraid you'll have to put up with a lapse or two on my part.'

'I...what were you going to do if I *had* been her...your elusive Miss Smith?' she asked nervously.

'Why do you ask?' Quick suspicion leaped into his world-weary eyes, and Helen realised wryly that he still wasn't *quite* convinced.

'Because I...Greg...' She faltered to a stop as he made the connection, and studied her thoughtfully.

'Ah, I see. So Greg told you what happened between us?'

'Of course he did. Greg and I are totally honest with each other.'

His eyebrows rose sceptically. 'But are you honest with yourselves?' he asked cynically. 'So, you're worried that I might want to stir up trouble for your valiant fiancé...extract a little belated revenge by claiming to have been a previous lover of yours?'

She shook her head. 'Is that what you were going to do?'

'*Are* you her?'

She was getting sick of denying it. 'No!'

He gave her a heavy-lidded smile, full of taunting secrecy. 'Then I guess we'll never know what I might have done, will we?'

Helen stiffened, not trusting that unreadable smile. 'It was so long ago...'

'Unfortunately...and sometimes fortunately, our memories are often independent of our wills,' Alex replied softly, and this time Helen knew that he wasn't thinking about his brother at all, but about the woman who had, in one night, apparently so captured his imagination. She must have been a dynamite lover! Helen shifted nervously under the sensual stare which actually didn't see *her* at all, but another...Helen ruthlessly crushed a fleeting envy.

'Alex——'

'*Alex!*' Another voice overrode hers. His mother's...floating up the stairs and through solid walls, as maternal calls do.

The tension was broken and Alex grinned. 'Mothers have a way with names, don't they? A certain pitch that, whatever you're being called for, makes you think, "Oh hell, what does she want me to do *now*?"'

'A very comforting familiarity, though, however old you are. I still miss my mother. I was her baby until the day she died, even though I was eighteen and living away from home.' She smiled warmly. 'Your mother is a fine substitute...hasn't got the pitch quite right, but near enough.'

'She obviously likes you enormously, she sang your praises in the letter that came with the photograph of you and Greg. I'm sorry if I've made you uncomfortable, Helen. I guess I should be relieved that I made a mistake.' He bent and brushed his mouth against her cheek. Helen felt the jolt right down to her toes. He drew back hesitantly, and frowned at her. He looked at her mouth and she *knew* what he was thinking. He was wondering again...wondering if she would taste the same as the woman whose image she was...

'No, Alex.'

His dark eyes flashed to hers at her stern command. 'We seem to be on the same wavelength, Helen. I didn't actually say a word,' he said with soft slowness. 'I was only thinking...'

'And I said *no*!' she fiercely denied sharing his impulsive thought.

'Alex? You are coming down for that drink, aren't you?' Once again Hannah's mother-summons came to the rescue.

'You'd better go,' urged Helen shakily. 'Hannah's dying to hear your news. I'll be down when I've done one or two things.' First of which was to pull her thoughts together. She must be missing Greg more than she had realised.

'All right. I suppose there'll be plenty of other opportunities over the next few weeks for us to get to know each other better.' He smiled that meltingly sexy smile and Helen's spirits quailed. That was what she was afraid of!

She frowned at him impatiently, and he threw up his hands, backing away. 'I'm going, I'm going.' His wicked smile became tinged with a faintly bitter irony. 'I'd hate to have Mum come up and find you hopelessly compromised by my company in your bedroom.'

'No one compromises me unless I want to be compromised,' she warned him categorically. So why, then, did he seem to take it as a promise?

'I'll remember that,' he murmured as he saluted her with a long, assessing look.

Helen moved restlessly around the room when he had gone. She had a nasty feeling that, in some unrecognised way, she had compromised herself already. What was it about Alexander Knight that so undermined her confidence?

Oh, Greg, my love, hurry home!

CHAPTER TWO

DINNER was an uncomfortable affair. There was no doubt that Hannah and Nicholas were delighted to have Alex home, but once their shock had worn off there was a constraint in their manner that it took Helen a little while to place. Then she realised that, other than a brief mention that Greg was in Sydney for a couple of days, they were careful to steer the conversation well away from their younger son, a noticeable omission when his fiancée was sitting at the same table. Could it be that they feared Alex's motives for his unexpected visit were not entirely cordial?

Alex didn't relieve their faint anxiety when he was purposefully evasive about the new book he had claimed he wanted to work on during his visit.

'Right now it's just an idea, I don't know if it'll work out or not. Actually, the main reason I came down was to get away from the rat-race for a while. The wedding was a good excuse.' His eyes flickered to Helen, who immediately dropped hers to her plate. 'I want to take it easy for a while...'

'You're not ill or anything, are you, Alex?' His mother was concerned.

'No, of course not,' he soothed, shrugging easily. 'I told you, I just wanted a break.'

Hannah and Nicholas accepted this with dubious smiles. Helen shared their doubt. In spite of his jet lag Alex radiated a restless energy that hungered for action. He was not a man who thrived on rest. Even as a child, Hannah had once confided to Helen when comparing the brothers, Alex had refused a daily rest. The inquisitive, determined and super-active child had become an equally active adult. 'Even when he was thinking...and he was a very intelligent, thoughtful boy...he had to be *doing* too.' Hannah had sighed reminiscently. 'I think that's what makes him such a uniquely gripping writer, his sheer *energy*...it leaps off the paper at you and shakes you to attention.'

'I thought you enjoyed the rat-race,' said Nicholas mildly. 'You certainly run against some pretty glamorous rats for some fairly glittering prizes.'

Alex's wicked, witty reply made his parents laugh. Helen studied him from underneath her lashes, trying to remember what else she knew about the man who had intruded so alarmingly into her life.

At thirty-six Alexander Knight was considered to be at the peak of his intellectual powers, but even the critics agreed that there was no knowing, given his past record, what new heights he might aspire to.

Little more than ten years ago he had been merely a highly respected New Zealand journalist but, following the break-up of his marriage, he had left the country to become a roving foreign correspondent for an Australian newspaper chain. He had made his name internationally with an exclusive story on the ruthless hijacking of a plane on which he had been a passenger. Fleet Street had beckoned and over the next few years Alexander Knight's by-line had appeared in newspapers all over the world. Wherever there was a coup or a war or a catastrophe, Alex was in the thick of it, still finding time in between to produce a string of enormously successful thrillers filled with sex and violence and a pervasive pessimism about the future of mankind that Helen had found extremely disturbing.

He had lived up to his image, too, as a hard-bitten man of action, in a lifestyle that, as one reviewer snidely put it, 'made Norman Mailer look like a celibate'.

Then, suddenly, Alexander Knight had dropped out of sight. Speculation was that he was involved in some delicate undercover investigative journalism, but when he re-emerged into society again it was empty-handed, and there were rumours that he had burnt himself out. Certainly he showed no signs of taking up his career as a correspondent again. Instead he seemed to be content to enjoy spending his accumulated wealth and shrugged off any questions as to where he had been in the preceding six months.

A month later all attention was on a new author, Stephen Errant, who had exploded on to the bestseller lists with a book that, as rarely happens, appealed to readers and critics alike. It was a lyrical novel of love, of the strength and frailty of the human spirit, the story of a man's journey out of the darkness of unspeakable despair into the light of freedom—physical, emotional and spiritual. It was hailed as an intellectual *tour de force*, and yet its style and plot and beautiful characterisations made the story accessible to millions of readers who would never dream of considering themselves 'intellectual'. The style defied definition, standing as it did astride dream and reality, the elusive heroine of the title, the man's *Angel in the Dark*, someone who might or might not have actually existed except in the hero's mind.

It was only when all the reviews were in, universally favourable, that the identity of the hitherto publicity-shy author had been announced: Alexander Knight. There had been howls of outrage from the critics, even one or two suggestions that it was all a ruse, that Knight was just acting as a front for the real author, but the reviews stood, and for most people Knight and Errant were too much of a coincidence.

The rumours were quelled by his second novel, a year later, this time published under his own name. Entirely different from *Angel in the Dark*, it had an equally powerful impact on the literary scene. Both books had won several literary prizes, and his third book, published the previous year, was also an instant bestseller.

It felt odd to sit across the table from a man who had been called a literary giant. In spite of the kind of life he led, Helen couldn't see any overt signs of dissipation. His skin was tanned and taut and, having changed into a white shirt and dark trousers for dinner, he displayed a suppleness of body that bespoke a surprising fitness. Mind you, Helen's thoughts drifted into deep waters, his bedroom athletics probably kept him in good shape!

Her eyes wandered up over his open collar and the strong tanned throat as his attention shifted and he caught her staring. Helen found it impossible to look away this time. Heat roiled in her belly. There was a leap of emotion behind the watchful dark eyes, a sudden focusing that sent a frisson up her spine.

'Not hungry?' The resonances of his warm, slow voice echoed oddly in the corners of her mind.

Helen was surprised to see that she had been abstractly pushing her food around her plate. 'Not really.'

'Perhaps you're pining for Greg.'

Was he being snide? Helen gave him the benefit of the doubt. 'I'm not the type to pine for what I can't have,' she said pleasantly.

'"What's gone and what's past help should be past grief"?' Alex murmured with familiar ironic lift of his eyebrows, and she realised that he had taken her words the wrong way, as a dig at himself. For a cynic, he was damned sensitive, she thought irritably.

'It's my cooking that she doesn't have much of an appetite for,' Hannah rushed into the silence, smiling nervously at her son's closed expression. 'Helen disapproves of all the cholesterol and additives that go into my meals.'

'You're a wonderful cook, Hannah,' Helen protested sincerely, 'This chicken casserole is delicious. I simply prefer small helpings, that's all.'

'Alcohol can be fairly damaging too, but you don't seem to have any objection to that.' Alex indicated her empty glass. He had produced a bottle of champagne, chilled for him on the plane, from his hand-luggage, and opened it with a speedy lack of flourish that bespoke long experience.

'I don't object to anything in moderation,' she said demurely.

'Moderation in all things?' An edge of sarcasm threaded the comment. 'What a paragon Greg has found himself.'

'Actually, I found *him* . . . and I wasn't even looking,' Helen said truthfully. She had had lots of plans for her life, marriage being only one of them, but she also knew that regrets were more often the result of what one *didn't* do than what one did. She had fallen in love with Greg so quickly and totally that it had to be fate. She would have been a fool to dither just because she had thought she wasn't ready to settle down just yet. For Helen, the present was more important than the future, for who knew how long that future would be?

Hannah cleared her throat. 'I told you in my letter, didn't I, Alex, that Helen knits? Her latest set of designs featured in an edition of Australian *Vogue*. She does these really marvellous sweaters . . . she's even managed to get your father into something verging on the trendy, one with fruit trees all over it. She's very clever at matching people to her designs. Nick, being the rabid conservative that he is, didn't like it at first, but lately he's been actually putting it on voluntarily, haven't you, Nick?'

'Only because you gave all my good old jumpers to the jumble sale,' growled Nicholas, and Helen shared a secret smile with him. His sweater had been a birthday gift from his wife, but what Hannah didn't know was that Helen had discussed the design with her husband first because she hated her craft to be wasted. Nicholas was a keen orchardist, proved by the mass of spring-blossoming trees in the huge back garden, and he had been pleased at the cunning pattern that Helen had come up with against a soft green background. He had been stubborn about wearing the sweater initially because Hannah would have been suspicious about her 'surprise' if he had taken to it straight away, since Nick had a reputation for clinging to old clothes as if they were family heirlooms.

'I could do with a new one myself,' said Alex, quick to observe and appreciate the silent communication that took place over his mother's head.

'Why don't you get Helen to knit you one while you're here?' said his mother, taking up the unravelled thread of his conversation. 'Could you do that, Helen? Think what a wonderful advertisement to have Alexander Knight walking around in one of your jumpers.'

'I'm up to my eyes in work already,' Helen said, strangely reluctant.

'New York winters can be really bitter,' her reluctance prodded him into saying plaintively.

'Do you stay there in the winter?' Helen asked, wondering why he was bothering to persist. 'I got the impression that you usually spend your winters with . . . I mean, somewhere warm.'

'With someone warm?' he capitalised on her slip with wicked swiftness. 'You seem to know an awful lot about me for someone who's only just been introduced.'

'Now, Alex, don't try and embarrass Helen,' his mother admonished. 'Your private life isn't exactly much of a secret.'

'Oh, but it is.' His eyes glinted with wry self-derision. 'You see, my private life is lived almost entirely up here.' He touched his lean temple. 'It's my public life that excites all the speculation, and since it helps sell books . . .' He shrugged and speared Helen again as she was just about to relax. 'I promise I'm not the notorious rake and libertine they make me out to be, Helen. Won't you please keep me warm this winter?'

His parents laughed at his teasing, but Helen could only manage a thin smile. She didn't like him flirting with her, her uneasiness increasing by the minute.

'What sort of design do you think you might like?' she asked. If she put him off long enough, he might forget about it.

His eyes were hooded. 'How about a halo?'

'On *you*?'

'Mmm . . . on a black background. Appropriate, isn't it? I could say I'm looking for an angel to fit it. It would give me a perfect excuse to go around clutching women to my manly chest.' She glared at him and he laughed. 'Only clutching, I promise, and if they didn't fit I'd throw them instantly away.'

'My sweaters are expensive,' she warned, mentally adding a hefty weighting for nuisance value. If she *had* to knit him something, he could pay through the nose for it.

'Price is no object,' he said blandly, reading her expressive eyes. 'It's the thought that counts, not the cost.'

'It counts to Helen,' his father said. 'She saves all her money to spend on her travels. Loves to travel, don't you, Helen? Been all over the place, haven't you? Europe, Asia . . .'

'But not Hong Kong?' Alex directed the casual enquiry more towards his parents than Helen, trying to catch her out in a lie.

'Not Hong Kong,' said Helen firmly.

'Not yet,' supplied Hannah happily, 'but you'll want to go some time to visit your sister and her children, no doubt.'

'Sister?' Alex's voice sharpened. 'I thought you said she lived in the States, or do you have more than one?'

Helen didn't flinch under the black-eyed stare. 'No, Susan is the only sister I have. Her husband works for a multinational chemical company, and they tend to move around. At the moment he's stationed in Hong Kong.'

'Is that the first time she's been there?'

'Yes,' said Helen tersely. She knew what he was getting at and she didn't like it.

'Except for that short time she was there when she was ill,' said Hannah, rising to collect up the dinner-plates. There was a small, electric silence following her innocent statement.

'Yes, but that was only for a few weeks,' Helen managed to say, fighting her guilt. She had genuinely forgotten but, of course, Alex wasn't going to believe that.

'Ill in Hong Kong?' he murmured. 'That must have been expensive.'

'The company covered the medical costs. Susan and Jack had been in the process of moving from Germany to the States, and they went via Singapore and Hong Kong because Jack had business there. Sue came down with an ear infection in Hong Kong and couldn't fly, so she had to stay on there for three weeks.'

'When was that, exactly?' asked Alex, politeness masking his intense interest.

Helen shrugged. 'Several years ago.'

'You said it was when you went to England, so it would have been five years ago, wouldn't it?' said Hannah.

'How old is your sister? Does she look anything like you?' Alex asked grimly, and Helen felt his controlled anger like a spur.

'Not really. She's four years older than me. And five years ago she was pregnant with her first child!' *That* should put paid to his ridiculous speculations.

'How pregnant?' was all he asked.

She wondered if she should lie. 'Three months,' she said reluctantly. His eyebrows rose and she glared at him.

'If you're not going to eat any more of that, I'll clear it away.' Hannah interrupted the silent exchange as she reached for Helen's plate. 'I've got just the dessert for you, Helen—fresh fruit salad. No, don't get up, I can manage...'

'Why so interested in Susan?' asked Nicholas as his wife bustled out of the room.

'Because, if she looks very much like Helen, I think I might have met her in Hong Kong five years ago.' Helen was horrified. Surely he wasn't going to tell the story to his *father*? 'I thought it was Helen herself at first, but she tells me I'm wrong.'

'Oh.' Nicholas's eyes darted from one to the other, and he looked briefly disturbed. 'Where did you think you met?'

'At a party——'

'It wasn't my sister,' said Helen tautly.

Alex shrugged. 'If you say so.'

'I do. My sister happens to be deeply in love with her husband, and she was over the moon about being pregnant that first time.'

'We often think that we know those closest to us,' Alex commented with a sharply cynical half-smile. 'But they're in the best position of all to blindly deceive.'

'Alex!' Nicholas admonished warily, and Alex leaned back in his chair to reassure carelessly,

'It's all right, Dad, I'm not going to rake over cold ashes.' To prove it, he threatened Helen with a charming smile. 'So, you like to travel. When you were in Europe, did you get as far as Greece?'

The innocuous topic of foreign customs took up the rest of the meal, with Alex entertaining them with horrendous stories of the complications he had encountered in his career. He still travelled a great deal, but these days as a 'peace correspondent', as his former colleagues jokingly called him.

They moved from dining-room to lounge for tea and coffee, and the talk drifted from Alex's loose schedule of interviews and public appearances over the next two weeks to the arrangements for the wedding. Alex idly asked who Greg had chosen for his best man, and his parents exchanged uneasy glances.

'Well, Greg hasn't got anyone yet. After he knew you were coming...he thought, he wondered...' Hannah looked pleadingly at her husband.

'He thought you might agree,' Nicholas finished. 'After all...' he trailed off, a faint flush rising under the leathery complexion.

'After all, he was best man at mine,' murmured Alex, the hard, cynical note back in his voice. Helen sat very quiet, surprised that Greg hadn't mentioned his thought to her, and even more surprised that he had been Alex's best man, in spite of their bitter estrangement at the time.

'I suppose he asked you to sound me out,' Alex continued draining his champagne glass with a restless flick of his wrist. 'Typical Greg, still trying to duck his responsibilities.' He switched his black-eyed stare to Helen, as if daring her to defend her fiancé. Prudently she remained silent, knowing that she would only make things worse by entering the fray in what was purely a family matter. And, whatever Hannah said, Helen wasn't a member of the family yet.

'He wasn't sure how you'd feel,' said Hannah gently, not denying his first comment. 'He was worried you might feel offended if he didn't ask, but that if he did you might——'

'If he wants to know how I feel, he can ask me himself,' said Alex tautly.

'But...'

'Alex is right, Hannah,' said Nicholas quietly. 'We shouldn't have mentioned it. It's between Greg and Alex.'

'I'm glad you did,' said Alex, adding a dash of cream to his coffee to bring it to the colour of his shuttered eyes. 'It gives me some idea of what's in his mind these days.'

'But... will you do it?' his mother persisted, obviously torn between her two sons.

Alex looked at Helen and her hand clenched unconsciously around her coffee-cup. 'I'll think about it,' he said briefly, and this time his mother knew to leave well enough alone.

Helen helped with the dishes, leaving the two men talking, and lingered in the kitchen afterwards as Hannah laid a tray for supper. Four cups. Helen nibbled her lip. Unfortunately it had not been her Saturday for the shop, and she had done nothing but a little light housework at home all day, so she could hardly slink off to bed early pleading tiredness. But nor did she look forward to a cosy foursome in the lounge, trying to ignore the unsettling effect that Alex had on her.

She compromised by fetching her knitting bag, which always accompanied her. She wouldn't get out the cardigan she was knitting for Susan's youngest, six-month-old Carolyn, because she didn't want the subject of her sister and Hong Kong to rear its ugly head again, so she sat safely in the big, fat, floral easy-chair in the lounge, while Alex and his mother shared the settee and his father puffed his pipe in the padded rocker, and worked on an intricate patchwork design in supersoft mohair for a television commercial.

Hannah was on the way to the kitchen to put on the kettle when the telephone rang.

'It's for you, Helen,' she came back to tell her, adding unnecessarily, 'It's Greg, from Sydney.'

Helen hurried out, feeling Alex's gaze tingling between her shoulderblades. She hoped her relief wasn't too evident in her voice as she talked eagerly to Greg, feeling the familiar and immensely reassuring rush of love.

'I miss you,' she said impulsively, and he laughed.

'Good. I'm missing you, too.' There was a slight pause in which Helen could hear the buzzing of the line. 'Mum told me Alex is there.'

'Yes.' Helen didn't quite know what to add, what he expected her to say. 'I was here when he arrived. He flew all the way from New York, so I think he must be pretty tired, although he hides it well.'

'Alex always did have incredible stamina.' Greg's voice sounded so dry, Helen wasn't sure whether it was a compliment or a criticism. 'Has he said anything about me?'

'No, not really,' said Helen awkwardly. Should she tell him about the misunderstanding about her double? She decided there was little point mentioning it over the phone. 'I...your mother did mention about the best man...'

'Oh...yes, well...I thought it would be a gesture...you know. What did he say?' he asked uneasily.

'That he'd think about it. He said you should ask him yourself.' And Helen agreed with him, although she didn't say so.

There was another small, buzzing silence. 'Oh, well...I guess we'll talk it over when I get back. I'll be flying in tomorrow evening now, not on Monday morning, so how about we go out for dinner?'

'Lovely.'

'I'll call you when I get in. 'Bye, darling, I love you.'

'I love you too, Greg.'

She hung up with a dreamy smile on her face.

'Do you?'

The soft query tugged her around. Alex was there, in the half-shadow thrown by the stairs.

'Very much,' Helen told him proudly.

'Lucky Greg. And does he love you, "very much"?'

She resented his mockery. 'Of course, we wouldn't be getting married otherwise.'

'Why the big rush? Mum says you've only known each other a couple of months.'

'Because neither of us sees any reason to wait.'

'Of course, there are other reasons for getting married,' he said, sauntering into the light, 'other than love.'

'Are there?' She refused to play his game, to be the mouse to his cat.

'You could be pregnant.'

'I could be,' she lied, 'but I'm not.'

'You could be dazzled by his wealth.'

'He works hard for it,' she clipped. 'As you pointed out yourself, money really isn't that important. Greg has plenty going for him without it—he's handsome, clever, charming... and he doesn't have to go around trying to scrape acquaintances with people by claiming to have met them before.'

The sting in her comment amused rather than annoyed him. 'What about sex?'

'What about sex?' said Helen aggressively, trying not to blush.

'It sounds as if you were both swept off your feet. Perhaps you're mistaking physical attraction for something deeper.'

'Thank you, but I think we're capable of deciding our feelings for ourselves,' Helen snapped, furious at his presumption. 'There's a great deal more to our relationship than the kind of casual encounters *you're* used to.'

'Helen——' He reached out and gently stopped her as she would have stomped back to the lounge. 'I'm sorry.' His hand left her arm reluctantly and combed tiredly through his thick, blond hair, leaving it unevenly spiked. He shook his head ruefully. 'I've apologised more to you in one night than I have to any other woman in my whole life. I know I'm coming on strong but... perhaps it's just that, having a failed marriage behind me, I'm too aware of the pitfalls. Being "in love" with someone is totally different from *loving* them day to day. Don't make the same mistake I did.'

Helen felt herself weaken, although she knew that there was far more than just his marriage behind his remarks. Under the harsh hall light he looked weary...disillusioned...vulnerable. She glimpsed a fleeting loneliness that almost frightened her, and a correspondingly frightening desire to try and ease it. Goodness, Alexander Knight was one man who would never need to be lonely!

Later, ready for bed in a nightgown that Hannah had made for a niece whose birthday was coming up—a demure thing in thin sprigged cotton—Helen knew that she had been unfair. The more intelligent the man, the greater his capacity for loneliness, and no one could deny that Alex was not acutely intelligent. A man didn't move through life in the kind of searching, restless way that he did if he wasn't seeking something that he felt was lacking in his existence.

She opened the small dormer windows under the sloping roof and enjoyed the fragrance of the spring air for a few minutes before succumbing to a cracking yawn. She was just about to jump into the big, welcoming bed when she heard a soft tapping on the door. She smiled ruefully. She might not want to think about Alexander Knight, but his mother would. Hannah probably wanted to know what Helen thought of him. Helen wouldn't shock her by telling her!

It wasn't Hannah but the man himself, leaning against the doorjamb, almost falling into the room as she opened the door. His hand met the soft flesh of her half-bare shoulder as he steadied himself.

'Sorry.' His touch lingered as his hand fell and he straightened.

'What do you want, Alex?' she whispered, looking down the empty hallway.

'To say goodnight.' He took in her fresh-scrubbed look, the green eyes slanted in annoyance, the delicate hollows of her collarbone and the way the thin lawn

sheathed but didn't disguise her body. He was wearing
a white towelling robe that accentuated his tan, modestly wrapped over so that there was only a narrow slit
of chest showing, thickly covered with damp hair. No
swaggering about or flaunting his body for Alex ... he
didn't have to! He would be sexy in a suit of armour,
decided Helen sourly.

'Goodnight,' she said drily, not believing him. She
started to close the door, but he was too quick for her.
The sleeve of his robe fell back as he braced his hand
against the wooden panel, revealing a lean, hard forearm
glinting with blond, silky hair, the muscles clearly de-
fined by his action. Helen knew that his skin would feel
like hot satin and that his fingers were lightly calloused...

'Alex——' she protested at his action and her
thoughts.

'Was your sister blonde five years ago?'

'No! Alex, it wasn't me and it wasn't Susan. Why can't
you accept that?' Her voice vibrated with low anger.

'But she does have green eyes, like yours?'

'More grey than green, but——'

'And has she got an odd-shaped mole, at the top of
her thigh, on the left?' he asked with soft urgency. 'Just
here.'

'*No!*' Helen was pale with shock and outrage as she
struck his hand away. His brushing fingers had nearly
touched her intimately, burning through the thin
nightgown. 'She hasn't got any moles anywhere!' she
choked. 'For God's sake, Alexander, stop harassing me
or I'll start screaming the place down. Good*night*!' She
offered a swift kick to his shins and, as he stepped back
out of range, slammed the door gratefully in his face.
She locked it for good measure and leaned against it,
her heart thumping. After a moment of silence she heard
him move away down the hall.

Helen walked over to the mirror. Her oval face was
white, a stiff mask around glittering green eyes and a

tight, thin mouth. She felt weak and shaken. Slowly she drew up the hem of her nightgown. She wasn't wearing anything underneath, and for a long time she stood, shivering, staring at the crescent-shaped mole that nestled in the hollow of her left groin.

How had he known? What did it *mean*?

CHAPTER THREE

'YOU'RE quiet.'

'Mmmm?' Helen roused herself from deep thought and looked over at the man behind the wheel. His brown-eyed seriousness prompted her to try and shake off her introspective mood. 'I was just thinking...'

'About what?' Greg smiled as he turned his eyes to the road ahead, hearing the familiar note of teasing in her voice.

'Oh, inconsequent stuff...like how much I love you,' she said demurely, and laughed as he threw the car into an exaggerated swerve of disbelief.

As their laughter mingled, Helen felt herself relax. Of course she had done the right thing by not mentioning Alex's mistake and, anyway, it was too late to casually introduce the subject now. In the three days since Greg had returned from Australia, the brothers had established a tentative accord which Helen was loath to disturb in any way, even jokingly. She had the feeling that Greg wouldn't find Alex's claim to prior knowledge of his fiancée very funny, mistake or no, and since Alex had obviously shrugged the coincidence away she would be wise to forget about it, too. The shock that she had felt when he had mentioned her mole had faded very quickly. Since she *knew* she couldn't be Alexander Knight's memorable one-night stand, she could only privately marvel at the excessively long arm of this particular coincidence.

'I thought you might have been a bit worried about tonight,' Greg said, again catching her off guard.

'Why should *I* be worried?' Helen asked carefully, and when Greg shrugged with unaccustomed helplessness she interpreted the gesture with dismay. 'Greg...*you're* not worried, are you? About asking him to be best man? I thought that it was just a formality. I thought you two had a long talk last night and that everything was resolved.'

Greg's mouth tugged on a wry, downward curve. 'Oh, we talked, but not about anything really important. When I skated around the subject of, you know, whether he still blamed me for...for what happened, he said the past was over and done with, and if I wanted to dwell on it and let it influence my present life that was my problem, not his. I had to seek my own absolution, he said. He had. Now what in the hell does *that* mean? I still can't work it out!'

Helen didn't even want to try. She sensed depths to Alexander Knight that only the courageous and daring would want to explore. 'Well, that's good, isn't it? Maybe that's his way of telling you that it's not a case of blame any more. If he can dismiss it so casually, why can't you?'

'Because it wasn't casual!' They were both startled by the vehemence of his brief burst of anger. Greg quickly regained control of himself, sending Helen a small, apologetic smile, consciously loosening his fierce grip on the steering wheel as the car slid to a stop at a city intersection. 'Sorry, honey...it's just that it caused an enormous upheaval in our lives and I can't believe that he's forgotten. If he really thought it was over and done with, why won't he discuss it frankly, knowing it would ease *my* mind? And why am I still picking up these strange vibrations from him? Have you noticed the way he *watches* everyone around him, the way he watches *us*? It's damned unnerving.'

'Writers are supposed to be acute observers,' Helen reasoned. 'Watching people and the way they interact together is probably second nature to him by now.'

'Mmmm.' Greg didn't sound very convinced. 'You don't like him, do you?'

'What makes you say that?' She looked at him sharply.

'Just an impression. You're a little too polite for comfort.'

He sounded pleased, and Helen realised that no matter how much he wanted a reconciliation with his brother he would be quite happy for *her* to keep her distance.

'I don't know whether I like him or not,' she said quietly, with perfect truth. She wasn't going to be maneuvered into expressing an opinion that wasn't hers, just to reassure Greg. She wondered if even he knew how he really felt about his brother. Pride and envy, respect and resentment seemed to create a certain ambivalence in his attitude.

'Anyway,' she said firmly. 'Alex would hardly have offered to take us out to dinner if he had it in mind to fling your overtures of friendship in your face. He strikes me as being very... frank.'

'Oh, yes, he's all for brutal honesty. But think of the convoluted plots he comes up with in his books. He's well capable of deviousness if it serves a purpose.' Again that mix of admiration and resentment. Glancing over and noticing her thoughtful expression, Greg strove to lighten the atmosphere he had created. 'Of course, Alex *could* be intending to walk out and leave me with the bill. Vichy prices are a revenge in themselves.'

Helen grinned. 'Somehow I can't see that impressing an old flame... if he's intending to fan any embers tonight!' The dinner was to be a foursome, Alex escorting a former colleague of his whom he had re-met at one of his scheduled interviews the day before.

'He wouldn't have to fan very hard,' said Greg drily. 'Sian was always crazy about him, right from when they started out in journalism together. Even after he was married she didn't give up. At one stage Alice was sure they were having an affair...'

His voice trailed off as he realised he had said more than he had intended to. Alice. Alex's former wife was almost never mentioned by the family, nor were there any photos of her in the family album. Idly Helen wondered what kind of woman the young Alexander had fallen enough in love with to marry, and the real reasons for the break-up.

'Ah, here we are.' Greg pulled his blue Jaguar over to the curb and turned off the engine. He unclipped his seat-belt and leaned over to give Helen a quick kiss. She responded warmly, as she always did, wanting to express the physical affinity she felt with him. When they had first met, Greg had been quite prepared to sweep her off into bed when she had shown herself willing, but when he had discovered that she was a virgin he had become touchingly chivalrous. He was an experienced man, he had told her gravely, and he didn't want to take the risk that his expertise might blind her to her true feelings. He wanted to be very sure that what she felt for him was truly love, and not just the first stirrings of womanly passion. Although Helen valued her virginity and was grateful that her love wasn't throwing her into conflict with her conservative upbringing, she couldn't help feeling a tiny bit piqued!

The restaurant interior was sophisticated and elegant, and Helen was glad that she had chosen to wear the red and gold silk dress, designed along the lines of a cheongsam, that Susan had sent for her birthday. In the back of her mind had been the thought that any old flame of Alexander Knight's was bound to be beautiful, and she didn't want to suffer too much by comparison.

She was right. She and Greg were having a drink at the small bar in the foyer when the other couple walked in. Alex, in pleated cream trousers and pale lemon, collarless knit shirt under a softly draped cream cotton jacket, made Greg's suit seem rather stuffy, as if *he* were the elder brother. Tanned and sexy, Alex turned every female head in the restaurant, and his partner was a perfect foil. As tall as he was, and very similar in colouring, Sian Miller was wearing a cool, white strapless dress which displayed her undeniably spectacular breasts to best advantage. Her hair was a tousled mass of curls which, natural or not, Helen instantly envied, for her own slippery-straight hair would never even hold a kink. The envy was mixed with an equally instant dislike, which wavered over the introductions when the beautiful, sexy sophisticate proved to be very humorous and down-to-earth.

As they progressed through a superb meal Helen was even able to feel a little bit sorry for her, for Alex, although responding to her flirtatiousness and joining her in fond reminiscence of their days as cadet reporters on the same newspaper, showed no signs of serious interest in renewing old affections.

Helen, who had reluctantly bowed to convention and allowed herself to be seated beside Alex, found her own expectations of the evening also unmet. Alex behaved like an impeccable brother-in-law-to-be, charming, interested, never once overstepping the bounds of politeness. So why couldn't Helen shake off her premonition of disaster?

She found out, half-way through her raspberry *torte*.

'Oh, by the way, Helen, I got our passports back from the consulate today, all stamped and ready to go,' Greg said, suddenly feeling in the inner pocket of his jacket. 'I meant to give it to you earlier.'

'You two going overseas?' asked Sian, switching her thwarted attention from an unresponsive Alex.

'Brazil, for our honeymoon,' grinned Greg.

'Sort of a working honeymoon,' teased Helen. 'Greg has some business there and I refused to let him go away without me so soon after the wedding.' She reached out to take the proffered passport, but Alex was too quick for her. When she protested at his hijacking, he raised his eyebrows.

'Have you got something to hide, Helen?' The lightly spoken mockery only thinly disguised the seriousness of his intent as he opened the small, stiff, dark blue booklet. 'Any secret trips to Columbia or the Golden Triangle you don't want us to know about?'

'Of course not.' She couldn't make a fuss now, without it appearing suspicious. She could hardly say that she didn't want him to see the horribly unflattering photograph of her. It had been taken when she was eighteen and planning her first trip overseas, to visit Susan and Jack in Germany. She looked thin and very young, all eyes and long, dead straight hair hanging down her back...like a wraith. She had been ill even then, but blessedly ignorant of the pain ahead which would force her to cancel her holiday.

'No distinguishing marks, if that's what you're looking for,' Helen said tartly, as dark eyes scanned the details printed next to the photograph. Thank goodness she hadn't listed that mole!

He smiled absently, leafing through the pages, now copiously filled with stamps. Thumbing back again, he stiffened. His smile chilled. 'I thought you said you'd never been to Hong Kong.'

'I haven't.' Helen knew a bluff when she heard one.

Wordlessly he handed over her passport, pointing to the page. There were two stamps there, both bearing the Hong Kong Immigration Service stamp. Helen felt her stomach clench around the riches she had over-indulged in. 'I...but that's impossible. I don't understand...'

'Perhaps someone stole your passport and used it, before politely returning it,' said Alex.

The hard edge of his sarcasm sliced through her bewilderment. She met his dark, accusing eyes. They made her feel hot and dizzy. 'There must be some mistake.' She looked pleadingly at her fiancé. 'I haven't been there, have I, Greg?'

'How would he know? Look at the date stamps,' Alex cut across his brother's attempted reply. 'It was before you and Greg ever met. Look at the *date*, Helen.'

She looked and felt panicky blackness dance across her prickling temples. *Five years ago.* She had been in Hong Kong five years ago, when Alex claimed he had met his mystery lover. For a moment Helen thought she was going to faint. Her lips moved without making a sound.

Greg gave his brother a furious look. He had known that the harmony was too good to last. Alex just couldn't resist making trouble, and over such an insignificant point. 'Here, darling, let me have a look.' He took the passport from Helen's numb fingers. His frown became a smile, the warm, loving, reassuring smile that wrapped itself around Helen like a security blanket. 'So you were in Hong Kong for a couple of days, and you don't re-member...it's not altogether surprising, considering the circumstances.'

'What circumstances?' Alex demanded.

'You're not on the job now, Alex,' Greg told him tightly. 'You don't have to act as if Helen is some kind of criminal obliged to defend her actions to the Fourth Estate.'

'I just find it odd that someone can forget an entire country.' Alex wasn't backing down an inch.

'Oh, I don't know,' Sian smiled warmly at the silent, pale Helen, trying to defuse the situation between the brothers. 'Hong Kong is hardly a country, more of a city state. There've been a few times and places *I* have trouble remembering...particularly when I've been having a good time.'

It didn't work. 'Selective amnesia, Helen? Blame it on the booze?' Alex's voice was as dark and bitter as his gaze, but Helen had no defence, she felt utterly sick and vulnerable.

'For your information, Alex,' Greg said, with coldly furious emphasis, 'Helen was seriously ill at the time she made that trip. If you look at the next stamp you'll see that Hong Kong was only a stop-over on the way to Britain. Helen was on her way to London for an operation, one that saved her life——'

'Greg!' Helen shook off her black horror, colour beginning to flood back into her pinched face as she felt the electric jolt of shock pass through the man sitting next to her, and heard Sian's soft sound of sympathetic curiosity.

But Greg ignored her muted protest. He was taking grim satisfaction in making Alex feel uncomfortable. It wasn't often that he got the chance to turn the tables on his brother, and he intended to make the most of it. 'No, Helen, for some reason Alex deliberately set out to make an issue of this, regardless of how upsetting he could see it was. Why should we consider *his* embarrassment? Helen had a brain tumour, not malignant, but the doctors here thought it was inoperable and it hadn't responded to chemotherapy,' he said bluntly, each word striking a blow for his pride. 'Fortunately, there was a new type of laser surgery being developed in London and Helen was considered an ideal candidate. The surgery was extremely accurate, but even so there was some peripheral damage...to her long-term memory. So you see, Alex, there's a perfectly reasonable and innocent explanation for Helen's forgetfulness.'

There was an awkward silence after his triumphant finish. Helen felt excruciatingly self-conscious, and furious with Greg. He hadn't been defending her as much as attacking Alex. He had been so intent on causing Alex embarrassment that he hadn't stopped to consider how Helen might feel, having a painful section of her past dished up with dessert.

'I'm sorry, Helen, I had no idea——'

'That's all right, Alex,' To Greg's chagrin, Helen interrupted the stiff apology. 'Of course you couldn't have known.'

'Next time, don't sit in judgement until you know the facts,' Greg sniped.

His brother ignored him. 'If you don't mind my asking, is the memory loss very extensive? Is it permanent?'

She did mind, but she couldn't very well say so without giving Greg another excuse for escalating hostilities. 'I only lost bits and pieces.' She managed a smile that avoided the dark, intrusive gaze, settling instead on Sian's more detached curiosity. 'Very disconcerting, especially if I don't know what they are. But I'm not aware of having any important gaps——' She stopped as she realised that that had suddenly become a lie.

'I suppose it depends on what one considers "important",' murmured Alex, and this time she did look at him, and was ensnared by the wry humour in his expression, the regret...a spark leapt across the silence and Helen's mouth went dry at the realisation: this man and she...

'Actually, the doctors said that it wasn't so much the actual memories that Helen lost,' said Greg, disgruntled by the way Alex had quietly manoeuvred out of his embarrassment, and aware that his own insecurities had got the better of him. Anxious to make amends to Helen, he explained diffidently to his brother, 'It was more the pathways to them—technically, the synapses between the neurons where memory is stored.' When Greg had originally learned of the illness which had been the impetus for Helen's wanderlust and determination to enjoy her life to the full, he had been concerned enough to do some research on the subject. Helen had lovingly tolerated his curiosity and fear, having coped with it all before. 'So everything is still there, probably, it's just that the proper pathways to the stored memories aren't there any more. The only way to get at them is to use an alternative pathway, sort of "re-wire" that section of the brain with new synapses. Isn't that the theory, Helen?'

Helen offered him a small smile of agreement, wishing fervently that he hadn't gone into such explicit detail when Alex asked the inevitable, 'And how does one go about "re-wiring" the memories?'

'By association of ideas. For instance, Helen found that she had forgotten the primary school she had gone to—it was just a blank, wasn't it? But she remembered bits of it when she smelled certain things—wet raincoats and wool—and she remembered the playground when she ate a banana sandwich. And hearing a voice that sounded like a teacher's voice triggered another memory. In the end the whole lot came back, once she had gained access to a certain number of associated memories...sort of like an avalanche building up...'

'Mmmm, there are a few things in my life I'd *prefer* not to remember,' Sian joked, sensing it was the right moment to inject a bit of humour. Unfortunately she chose something horribly appropriate for two of those listening. 'What a perfect excuse to claim ignorance of one's more ignoble actions!'

'Isn't it, though?' said Alex softly. 'However, you still have to cope with other people's inconvenient memories.'

Sian laughed and trotted out a few of her unflattering memories of Alex as an enthusiastic but grass-green cadet, and Helen felt the spotlight of attention shift with inexpressible relief. All she wanted to do was to go home and brood over the awful revelations of the evening, but to her horror the other three debated and decided to go on to a nightclub. While Alex went to pay the bill and Sian tracked down the ladies' room, Helen tried to plead tiredness, but Greg was adamant.

'I still haven't asked him about being best man yet,' he pointed out. 'I could hardly raise the subject after jumping down his throat about the passport thing. I shouldn't have let him get under my skin...sorry for coming over so heavy, darling, but I told you he makes me nervous. We won't stay long if you're tired, I promise, just enough for him to mellow out and agree how well matched we are, on and off the dance-floor!'

The nightclub which Sian chose to lead them to wasn't the loud, crowded, frenetic type of 'in place' that Helen had expected one with her showbusiness connections— Sian wrote for the entertainment section of a daily newspaper and freelanced on the subject for various magazines—to come up with. Rusty's obviously catered for the mature, sophisticated crowd who didn't care for games of show-and-tell. The drinks were still predictably overpriced but the music was at a level that encouraged comfortable conversation, a mixture of fast modern and slow 'smooch' which catered to all tastes. Immediately they sat down Sian was up again, dragging an amused Alex out on to the floor for a slow number, draping herself unselfconsciously over his lean, supporting body with sultry optimism.

'I wonder if Mum and Dad will see him home tonight?' grinned Greg as, not to be outdone by Alex who had ordered Château-Margaux at dinner, he asked for a bottle of champagne to be sent to their table. 'I get the feeling that Sian has other plans for him.'

He obviously believed that Alex would be mad not to fall in with them. Helen looked down and was surprised to see her hands clenched in her lap. Had it only been her imagination that sensed Alex's total disinterest in the other woman? Wishful thinking?

Out of the corner of her eye she noticed Alex catch a downward-straying feminine hand, and deftly began steering his partner back towards the table. Panic fluttered in her chest. She ignored the glass of champagne being poured in front of her.

'Let's dance, too!' she announced.

'Can't wait to be in my arms, huh?' Greg's brown eyes twinkled. 'OK, let's show 'em how it's *really* done...'

Greg was an excellent dancer, and Helen floated safe and secure in the knowledge that their steps meshed perfectly. How lucky she was to have fallen in love with a man who suited her so well in every way. Well, almost every way. Her linked arms tightened briefly around his waist as she felt a surge of resentment at Greg's scruples, and her own. She wished that they were already lovers, that she already belonged to him. *The way that she had once, briefly, belonged to his brother*... She wrenched her thoughts away. In spite of everything there was no evidence, just hearsay. It *couldn't* be true!

'May I cut in?'

It wasn't a request but a demand, and moments later Helen was matching steps with Alex, chagrined to find the smooth flow of movement undisturbed by the changeover of partners. She stiffened automatically against the hand on the curve of her back, but Alex made no attempt to pull her closer. His body kept a decorous distance, his right hand only lightly clasping her left. Too late, she realised why. It meant he had a square view of her face.

Her eyes flickered to his. There was no triumph in the darkness there, only a bleakness that was at odds with an unmistakable tenderness. She felt a curling in her stomach.

'Alex——'

'What are the chances of a recurrence of your illness?'

It was no use trying to fob him off. The first lesson a reporter learned was persistence. 'About the same as yours,' she said huskily.

He closed his eyes, thick golden-brown lashes trembling for a moment against the darkly tanned cheek.

Helen stumbled slightly, made weak by this show of weakness.

'Alex——'

'Greg said your parents died when you were seventeen; was there someone else here for you? Did your sister come over to be with you?'

Helen shook her head. 'I wouldn't have asked her. They were still in Germany at the time, and Susan was suffering the most horrendous morning sickness. She could hardly move out of bed. There'd been some bleeding early on, too, and she was worried about the baby.'

'So you didn't tell her anything,' he guessed rawly. 'You didn't tell them you were ill until...when?'

Under his gentle but inexorable questioning, Helen told the bare facts: the headaches that had got worse, not better, after her GP had diagnosed a virus, the long series of tests that had at first revealed nothing, the CT scan that had finally revealed the tumour and the fruitless attempt to reduce the growth by using chemotherapy. It was only after the specialist had investigated her eligibility—since she didn't have any medical insurance that would pay for expensive treatments—for Government-sponsored surgery in England that she had called Jack and got him to cushion the shock to her sister.

Alex's empathetic reaction was almost frightening. Helen could *feel* the sympathetic vibrations flowing from his body into hers, the fear and the need that made her want to pull away, to run.

'So young, and so alone...'

'I had friends, Alex, and I wasn't a helpless *child*.' She braced herself against the tug of her emotions. 'In a way it did me good. It made me strong. It made me reassess what I wanted out of life. It made me appreciate the true value of things...like love.'

Ah, that got a reaction! Long fingers dug punishingly into her back, but Alex proved appallingly indifferent to the goad.

'But you didn't have love then, did you, when you most needed it? Someone to hold you when you were frightened and alone, someone to listen to all the dark thoughts.' His husky sensitivity caressed her resistance. 'And chemotherapy—I know what a multitude of horrors that word can cover.' As if he couldn't help himself, he brushed his hard jaw against the silky darkness of her hair. She picked up the tacit reference immediately.

'I had some nausea and lost a lot of weight, that's all. I didn't have radiotherapy so I didn't have the trauma of hair loss, although the drugs turned it pure——' She stopped on a gasp.

'White,' he supplied for her, looking down at her aghast face

'I forgot,' she said lamely. Or blocked it out...

'I knew it couldn't have been natural, not with your skin tones,' he said with the shadow of a smile that grew in wickedness. 'I thought your desire to be a natural blonde was rather carried to extremes.'

She blushed and glared at him, and he laughed. She was surprised how relieved she was to hear the sound. Perhaps now he too would be prepared to forget...

'Are you going to tell Greg?' he asked suddenly.

'Tell him what?'

He sighed. 'About what happened in Hong Kong.'

Her face stiffened. 'Why should I? I don't *know* what happened. I only have your word for it. That rather puts me in a vulnerable position, doesn't it? Why should I believe what *you* say?'

'Why don't you hear what I have to say, first? Aren't you in the least bit curious to know the how and the why and the where? You might not remember...yet...

but don't you think it might be wise to be prepared? That night, I was at a party——'

Helen's steps by this time were in a hopeless tangle. She tried to pull herself away from Alex and suddenly realised that the light clasp that locked hers had incredible tensile strength. 'Look, Alex, I appreciate your thoughtfulness,' she said with desperate sarcasm, 'but coincidences like this do happen. I had a fairly strict upbringing and I never chafed against the restrictions. In my book, sex and love and marriage are pretty well indivisible. I wasn't, and aren't, the type to go for one-night stands.'

'I told you before, it wasn't like that. And you must admit that, under the circumstances, it wouldn't have been unlikely that your normal standards wouldn't apply. A young girl, on the verge of womanhood, and conscious that she might never get the chance to truly *be* a woman...'

'But it *couldn't* have been me!' Helen's soft cry threw up the last barrier to belief. 'How could it have when I'm still a virgin?'

Alex's misstep tangled with hers. He swore and apologised, and looked down at her flushed confusion with an incredulity that changed to embarrassing amusement. 'Helen... you only *think* you're a virgin. I'm afraid the difference is a little more than academic.'

Helen was speechless, the core of her inner certainty suddenly revealed as hollow. Somehow, in spite of the evidence, she had thought she held the indisputable ace. She shook her head dazedly.

'All it means, Helen, is that you haven't been to bed with anyone except me,' he said gently, and somehow that managed to make it more indecent than ever. Her back was rigid with fury against his steely restraint. His expression grew grave at her stony resistance. 'Think about it, Helen. If you and Greg are saving up for a wedding night of tender, virginal bliss, you're both in for a big shock.'

'Shut up, Alex,' she grated, the blows now coming too fast for her to absorb. 'How dare you——'

'I dare because I care, and it's important for you to face facts. We were lovers, Helen, and whatever you prefer to forget, it was no passionless piece of sexual byplay. Have you ever read *Angel in the Dark*?'

'What?' She didn't believe that he was expecting literary criticism from him at a time like this. What an ego! 'No, I never got around to it!' she snapped with pleasure.

'Well, you should.' He smiled, his mouth crooked. 'It's about you.'

'*What?*' Her horrified cry drew the attention of everyone nearby, and Helen's body felt as if it had been dipped in boiling water. 'You wrote about *me*?' She lowered her voice to a furious croak.

'About us, actually,' he admitted without shame.

'You wrote about…about…?' She couldn't force her mouth to form the awful words.

'Our one-night love-affair…among other things. You inspired me that night, Helen. You brought me back to life both physically and creatively. You're the reason for the best work I've ever done. In a way the book was a gift to you, a homage to a woman I had no other way of thanking…until now.'

Oh, God, so now the whole world knew more about the encounter than she did! Helen could see and hear, but she couldn't credit what she was hearing.

'Why are you doing this?' she whispered shakily. 'What do you *want*? I can't help what's past and I don't see the point of dwelling on it.' She recovered some of her shattered composure as he merely looked down at her with that strange, whimsical smile. 'You shouldn't either. Please, can't you put Greg out of his misery? It's so unfair!' Her courage was growing by the second. 'All

it would take is a few words, but you won't give them
to him. You still want to make him pay. Well, not
through me you won't! It's not as if he blighted your
life or anything... you went on to marry someone else,
didn't you, after your fiancée ran off? Have you ever
considered that maybe Greg did you a favour, that maybe
you and your fiancée just weren't right for each other...?'

His head had jerked back as if she had clipped him
smartly on the jaw. 'Is that what he told you?' he asked
harshly, and her heart sank at the smouldering resentment that smoked behind narrowed black pupils.

'He didn't mean to fall for her,' she pleaded urgently.
'Do you believe that he deliberately set out to fall in love
with a woman who was promised to his brother?'

'No,' he said quietly. 'One never does.'

Her mouth froze in a rounded 'O'. His bitterness had
burnt out in a brief flare of remembered pain, and there
was no mistaking his meaning. He held her with his
hands, with his eyes, and with the force of feeling in his
quiet statement of resignation...the peaceful declar-
ation of war.

'No...oh, no. No, Alex.' Helen's head moved jerkily
from side to side.

'Yes.' His arrogance was back in full force, and she
remembered who he was...the fêted literary darling who
was accustomed to taking what he wanted and paying
for it with words. He had grown rich on his experiences,
seeking ever wilder, more dangerous ones...

'I don't know what game you're playing, but I'm not
joining in.'

'I want you back, Helen.'

'You never had me!' she denied.

'You think it's just coincidence that we met again while
both of us are still free? It's not coincidence, it's fate.'

'But I'm *not* free!' She gasped, clutching at him as
he suddenly whirled her around in a series of swift
movements that took them to the far side of a fluted

pillar across the room from where Sian and Greg were well into the champagne. How long had they been dancing? Helen had no idea...it seemed like an eternity. 'Alex——'

He tasted his name on her lips, kissing her with one hand still around her waist, splaying up towards her rigid shoulderblades, the other braced against the column, his wrist pressing snugly into the side of her breast. Aware of the indignity and futility a struggle would represent, Helen tried to think of something prosaic, like the fact that her red high heels were pinching...anything to fight off the electricity charging through her nervous system. His mouth was hungry, inventive...and by the time it lifted from hers she was thoroughly flushed and breathless, her breasts tight beneath the restrictive silk.

'Damn you, Alex, what did you do that for?' Her glazed green eyes glittered with furious excitement. She felt naked before his black gaze, seeing the reflection of her own wayward desire in his taut expression of satisfaction.

'Just prodding your sensual memory,' he told her softly. 'Trying to create a new pathway. Did you remember anything?'

Helen went simultaneously hot and cold. 'No, and I don't want to either, so keep away from me, Alex, keep away from *both* of us!'

'I can't do that, in all conscience, Helen,' he said with a gravity that made her feel even guiltier than ever. 'I can't let you make that mistake.'

The rest of the evening passed in something of a blur. Later, when Helen sorted through her impressions, she knew that Greg had been already tense when she and Alex finally got back to the table after their prolonged session on the dance-floor. He had looked at them both with sharp suspicion, as if he sensed something in the air, and Helen was grudgingly grateful to Alex for forcing her to stay on the floor until her hectic flush had died

down to a marble coolness which owed a certain amount
to shock.

The blow-up came when Greg, half-way through a
second bottle of champagne, asked Alex to be his best
man, with such diffidence that Helen could have kicked
him. It was as if he expected to be rejected, and he was,
but in terms that even Helen, braced for the worst,
thought were unnecessarily brutal.

'I've already been involved in one failed marriage,
Greg. I don't intend to be party to another,' said Alex
calmly. 'Second best is never a good basis to work on,
take it from me.'

Thank God Greg didn't stop to work that one out!
He went utterly white, and three minutes later he and
Helen were outside on the pavement.

Helen's head was pounding with tension by the time
she closed her apartment door behind him, not least because he had refused to discuss the incident. Pale and
tight-lipped, he had shrugged off her attempts at sympathy in a poor imitation of his brother's indifference.
'Well, that's that. I should have asked Doug Sellers in
the first place.'

Her heart ached for him. She knew that Greg felt
things deeply and that, despite his pessimism, he had
truly believed that Alex would come around. Helen knew
that she couldn't let him suffer in silence; he deserved
to know the truth.

But what *was* the truth?

And how could she bear to hurt him all over again by
letting Alex get in first with *his* version?

She had to *know*.

CHAPTER FOUR

HELEN heaved a sigh, frowning heavily as she shuffled the scraps of multicoloured cloth around on the small wooden table. She was in the process of designing a multi-media patchwork sweater, but her brain wasn't making the right connections.

'Rough night, huh?'

She looked up at the breezy young woman who had just come through from the shop into the tiny backroom. Nicola was a bouncy blonde to whom rough nights came rarely. Helen usually enjoyed the days that the two of them shared the running of their market outlet.

'Let's just say that it wasn't restful.'

Nicola operated mobile eyebrows. 'With a guy like Greg on a string, a restful night would be a bit disappointing, wouldn't it?' Her grin glowed with a healthy vitality that made Helen tired to look at her. Fortunately there wasn't time for Nicola to indulge in any further friendly investigation as the sound of delighted American accents filtered in through the curtain that screened off the workroom from their display of woollens.

'You can fill me in at lunch time,' the blonde told her as she bounced out to make use of her enthusiastic sales technique.

Helen shuddered at the prospect of trying to explain the sleepless hours that she had just endured. Her call to Hong Kong, which had seemed like a bright idea at the time, had proved a mistake. Half-past midnight in Auckland had proved to be family rush-hour in the Colony. Susan had been in the process of steering re-

63

luctant youngsters into bed while she and Jack got ready to go out for the evening.

Consequently, although she had been pleased to hear from her sister, Susan had been distracted and their conversation, of necessity, rather short.

Yes, Helen had stayed with them for a couple of days at the Hong Kong Hilton on her way to have her operation...well, with Susan, actually, because Jack had flitted off to Tokyo—he had been working out of the Hong Kong office temporarily, until Susan's condition had enabled her to continue on to their new home in America.

'The company were marvellous, actually—paid for everything. Anyway, I was practically a basketcase by then, worrying about my ears and you and the baby, and then you arrived and put me to shame. I mean, you were so thin and big-eyed and your *hair*...but you were so calm and cool and *brave* that I felt like a complete hysterical idiot. I think you were the one comforting *me* instead of the other way around. You were actually pretty good at the time—you had pills for the headaches and you were a tiny bit clumsy but, honestly, no more uncoordinated than me after a couple of gins. Why do you want to know all this, anyway?'

'I've just met someone who says they met me at a party up there...and I don't remember.'

'Oh, you mean you don't *remember*!' Susan understood immediately. She laughed. 'And here I was thinking that you were being frightfully discreet about your little fling...'

'Little fling?' echoed Helen hollowly, preparing herself for the worst.

'Mmmm, ouch! Sorry, just trying to pin my hair with one hand. I didn't dare go far from the hotel...I was still throwing up everywhere, and I didn't want you to miss out, you seemed so eager to fill up your days...so I jacked up some sightseeing for you, and on the second night you went out to some party that someone in the company had sent us invitations to and you didn't get back until it was nearly time for your flight...'

'Susan!' Helen was shocked at her sister's casualness, but of course, Susan had had five years to adjust. 'Why didn't you *tell* me?'

'Because I thought you knew, of course.' Susan's voice was impatient. 'What does it matter now, anyway? Water under the bridge.'

'But... weren't you worried, at the time, I mean?'

A grin came down the wire. 'Honey, the last thing you said to me at the airport was that the chemotherapy had made you "temporarily unable to conceive".'

'Oh, God!'

'And that I wasn't to worry about any "little consequences".'

'I can't believe I said that,' groaned Helen. She could never have been so cavalier.

'Oh, don't be such an idiot, Helen,' her sister reproved warmly. 'You were laughing, you were happy, you said that you'd had the most marvellous night of your life... you made me laugh instead of cry when I waved you off. What was there to worry about? You were nearly twenty, you were mature way beyond your years; I thought you deserved to have some fun, something to take your mind off what was ahead. If I'd known who the guy was I'd have given him a medal and to hell with Mama's homilies! Hey, Helen——' her voice sobered. 'You're not thinking about confessing this to Greg, are you? Big mistake, dragging up the past. And take my advice, don't ask *him* about past indiscretions, either... at his age, he's bound to have a few. A marriage doesn't need a load of excess baggage on board when it's taxiing for take-off! If you can't remember any of it yourself, what's to worry about, anyway?'

Not a reassuring conversation, thought Helen despairingly as she hung up the phone. She didn't feel like sleeping so she ran a hot bath and soaked in it for a while, but instead of it relaxing her, the watery brooding only made her more uptight. Thoughts scurried around in her brain like shell-shocked rats in a maze.

Ironically, she thought if she only *could* remember some of her five-year-old encounter with Alexander Knight, then she might be able to forget. It was the not knowing, the not understanding that was devastating. The awful feeling of being a stranger to herself. All this time Helen had thought of herself as a particular kind of person. She liked to live life to the full, to seek new experiences, but that had never included sex. That was an experience that she wanted to be special, to be *right*. She had been so busy with her travelling, her savouring of her health and freedom, that she hadn't had *time* to stay in one place long enough to develop a serious relationship with a man...until Greg.

Oh, God! Helen groaned out loud as she wrapped herself in a silky peach robe and glared at the clock in the kitchen as she boiled the kettle. One a.m. and she was still no closer to deciding what she ought to do.

If she told Greg the whole story, would he still want to marry her? And, if he did, would the knowledge that his brother had once been his wife's lover taint the whole of their future relationship? Would he ever be able to forget it? Given the way he felt about that long-ago upheaval with Alex, Helen was pessimistic.

On the other hand, if she didn't tell him and he found out, or Alex told him, she knew she wouldn't be able to lie and say that she hadn't known, even if she hadn't *remembered*. Helen was a hopeless prevaricator. Life was too short for lies.

So what should she do? Oh, damn Alexander Knight for getting in the way of her life! Damn him for not doing the decent thing and agreeing to be best man. What was she to him, anyway? Nothing! A character in some

story he had written. Well, he wasn't going to re-write
her life.

Even if it meant faking on her wedding night? Coffee
exploded from Helen's mouth as she choked on the realisation. Tears of pain and fury and frustration blurred
her vision as she gulped a cold glass of water to dislodge
the hard spasm of muscle in her throat.

When the doorbell rang she was glad for the dis-
traction. Anna must have got off her shift early—she
often swapped a few hours here and there with other
nurses—and forgotten her key. Efficient on the ward,
Anna was a chronic loser of keys and bags and articles
of clothing. Anna was also a good listener. Susan might
be flesh and blood, but she was either on a high, like
tonight, or a low; there were no sensible in-between's.
Anna specialised in sympathy in a wide range of greys.

It wasn't Anna. It was Alex. Still dressed in his pastel
finery, leaning tiredly against the whitewashed wall op-
posite her door, rough blond whiskers gilding his jaw.
He looked crumpled and slightly worn...and utterly
masculine.

'Don't you have a chain?' he growled at her speechless
shock. 'I could be some nutcase rapist.'

'This isn't New York,' she found her voice to respond
tartly, annoyed at being put on the defensive yet again.
She looked him up and down with shrivelling contempt.
'But I agree, you could. You certainly act like one. What
are you doing here, Alex? Do you know what time it
is?'

'It took me a while to shake off Sian,' he said, pushing
himself off the wall with a roll of his shoulders that
parted his jacket to reveal the lithe twist of muscles under
the thin fabric of his shirt. He sauntered across the
narrow stretch of hallway.

'I hope you didn't rush on my account,' Helen said
sarcastically. Had he succumbed to Sian's open invitation, after all? Her green eyes looked at him in dis-

taste. His mouth curved, and she realised what she had said. She had made it sound as if she had been *expecting* him to turn up on her doorstep. 'I don't know why you're here, but you can't come in!'

Her statement of unwelcome had no effect. 'I don't want to come in, I just came to drop this off.' He held out a book she hadn't noticed tucked under his arm, hidden by the soft folds of his jacket.

Helen recoiled from the glossy black cover with the embossed gold halo enclosing the title. 'You get me up at one o'clock in the morning to lend me a *book*?' she rasped incredulously.

He raised his eyebrows as his eyes fell, and Helen flushed as she realised she was still holding her half-empty coffee-mug. She thrust it behind her on to the telephone-table.

'Not lend. Give. It's your copy, Helen. It's gone everywhere with me in the last four years...just in case I should ever find you again. You might call it something of a talisman, a symbol of hope...'

If it had been anyone else Helen might have scoffed at such a line, but Alex made it sound appallingly natural. She wouldn't have been human if she hadn't been curious about what he had written about her, but it was a work of fiction. How much in there was fact and how much private fantasy? And how would she know which was which?

Slowly, reluctantly, she put her hand out. The dust-cover felt smooth and cool under her fingertips. The weight hurt her wrist so that she had to take it with both hands. All those words poured out on all those pages...Helen felt more apprehensive still, and it showed.

'What was the rush? Couldn't this have waited until morning? I won't have time to read it for a while anyway,' she said, to make certain he knew she was not committing herself.

'Find time. You need to read it.'

'You know nothing about my needs,' she told him fiercely, and thick, warm brown lashes screened his eyes as they dipped to wander down over the silken drape of her robe, making both of them aware that she could be wearing nothing underneath, and that her skin was still slightly damp from her bath. The fragrance of the Chanel body lotion that Greg had bought her the last time he was in Singapore hung in the air between them, the scent of femininity. *Greg.*

'Don't, Alex,' she warned him thickly, clasping his book to her breasts to crush the treacherous tingling she felt there.

As if he knew what she was trying to hide from him, he smiled wryly. 'Just looking,' he murmured, and the words slid over her hot skin like a caress and made her more aware of her vulnerability than ever.

'Well, don't!' she said flatly. 'Haven't you done enough to Greg for one night?'

His face tautened, the dark eyes taking on a hooded fire. 'Would you prefer me to be a hypocrite? I'm not a religious man, Helen—at least not in the conventional sense of the word——' No, there was nothing at all conventional about Alexander Knight! '—but I don't mock the genuine beliefs of others. And my agreeing to support Greg in church would be a mockery. This *marriage* is a mockery.'

'I happen to love Greg and he loves me. We want to spend the rest of our lives together, raise a family,' she hurled at him furiously, outraged by his presumption, his smugness! 'Perhaps you find it difficult to understand the concept of permanence in a relationship, but——'

'Oh, I not only understand, I subscribe to it. I've been faithful to you, Helen, to the memory of what we shared.'

Helen struggled for breath as she absorbed the impact of his words. She laughed a little wildly. 'If you're trying to tell me that——'

'I haven't made love to a woman for five years. You've been celibate for that length of time, why shouldn't I be?'

It was too absurd for words. She gaped at him, hot colour pouring into her face.

'Because I'm a man?' He made the sexist jeer softly, inviting her to reject the old double standard.

'Because you're Alexander Knight!' she spat at him. It was imperative that she not believe him. 'You've had a string of girlfriends as long as this book!' She shook it in his lying face. 'I suppose you're going to claim they all wanted you for your mind, not your body!'

He shrugged, eyes glinted at her small, fiery face. 'You might find me irresistibly sexy, darling, but other women do respond to me on other levels, you know.'

'Why, you——'

'I won't deny plenty of women have tried, but frankly, Helen, I've been too busy writing to take up the offers.' He grinned virtuously at her snort, his voice lowering to a rusty velvet. 'Besides, once you've had the best, nothing else will do. I wasn't interested in sex because I knew it would be unfulfilling. It's easy to be celibate if there's no temptation, no desire.'

'Are you claiming you're impotent?' she demanded accusingly, uncaring of the bizarre intimacy of the conversation taking place in an open hallway.

'Oh, far from it...dreams of you kept me in functioning order,' he said wickedly. 'I didn't need other women, Helen, because I had you.'

'That's sick!' she choked, fancies dancing before her horrified eyes.

'Would you rather I had lived up to my reputation as a literary stud?' He shook his head. 'And this the woman who guarded her...er...dubious virginity so assiduously? You might have forgotten I existed, Helen, but I never forgot you. How could I? You cured me of a terminal sickness of the soul, performed a kind of sexual healing that made me realise how hollow and pointless the physical act is if it contains no kindness, no deeper need than the purely sexual, no sharing of one's essential self, black fears and all. I didn't *consciously* decide that I was going to give up sex altogether, it just happened that in the last five years I haven't met a woman who interested me more than my work, who moved me half as much as the way you did the first time I saw you.'

'I think you'd better go,' said Helen shakily, unable to cope with his intent seriousness. Intellectually he could tie her up in knots; emotionally... here she felt on very unstable ground... emotionally he frightened her. She half expected him to ignore her plea and push his way past her into the apartment, but as usual he disconcerted her by accepting her rejection quietly.

'Read the book, Helen. At least do that much.' The crooked smile appeared, that undermined her determination to dislike him. 'It might help you understand me, if not yourself. And I think you should examine, very carefully, your reasons for marrying Greg.'

He couldn't resist that, could he? 'I don't think I *want* to understand you.'

'I know. But you'll like the book, anyway. There's a lot of love in it.'

'You mean sex.' With her? She swallowed hard.

'Beautiful sex...' he mocked her unease. 'My angel does turn out to be human, after all. A flawed angel, with a mole just there...'

She should have jerked away, but she couldn't. His touch was like the stroke of a magnet against iron filings, dragging a riot of sensation to pool in the delicate hollow of her hip. She swayed. 'Alex——' Her voice ached with protest, more against herself than him.

'Don't worry, I won't hurt you. I learned something else these past five years. Patience,' he told her, his thumb moving softly against the slippery satin.

'But you *are* hurting me,' she cried out huskily, catching his wrists, feeling the power in the narrow band of bone and tendons as his hand twisted to entwine his fingers with hers.

'Life is pain. I'm just waking you up, that's all, Sleeping Beauty...reawakening you.' His lips were gentle against the side of her wrist, his head bent, eyes lowered, almost as if he was paying knightly homage, thought Helen, fighting a slipping sense of reality. He sounded almost submissive, but that was an illusion, she told herself, Alex was no tool of fate. Whatever his beliefs, he believed foremost in himself; she could not imagine him submitting easily to defeat. Alex was a natural-born fighter, and she sensed that resistance merely fuelled his enthusiasm for the chase, whether it be after a good story or a woman...

'This isn't a fairy-tale, Alex. I'm not under any wicked spell. I'm perfectly happy with my life...with Greg.'

'But that's because you don't know what you're missing...literally.' He laid her hand against the taut curve of his neck so that she could feel his disturbing words vibrating in his throat, a hum that echoed through her body. 'I know things about you that no one else does, not even you. I know what you're capable of, as a woman, and I think you deserve better than my brother.'

'I suppose you mean you!' Her scorn was rather too shaky to be effective, he was too clever at plumbing her doubts. 'Thank God, we rarely get what we deserve in this world. Let me go, Alex. I'm tired and I want to go to bed.'

'So do I,' he murmured, dreamy, speaking eyes telling her that he didn't have sleeping in mind. He took her hand from his throat as if he was going to give it back to her, and Helen's lips parted on a small sigh of relief that turned into a gasp as he jerked her forwards against his lean hardness and covered her mouth with his. Braced against the memory of his sensual onslaught on the dance-floor, Helen was almost undone when his kiss was slow and soft—no threat or urgency, just an intimate touching. Eyes closed against the consequences of even the slightest acquiescence, Helen let him impose his sweet will, feeling her nipples press painfully against the glossy hardness of the book she still clasped to her breasts.

'Read me,' he whispered against her tender mouth as he eased himself away, releasing a flood of shame that she could have, even for a moment, been unfaithful to her fiancé. 'Read me and remember...'

Oh, she had read him all right, Helen thought grumpily as she gave away the patchwork squares and decided to pick up her needles and finish off one of her more conventional efforts, a natural-wool cable-knit sweater that a customer was planning on mailing to a relative in England for a Christmas present.

Helen hadn't meant to read a line, but when she had recovered from Alex's abrupt departure she had flipped through the book, intending to browse, defiantly reading the last page, as if by so violating the integrity of the book she could deny its potency. The ending—as abrupt in its way as Alex's departure had been equally unsatisfying. Slowly, under the guise of 'browsing', Helen had retraced through the book to the shock of the dedication page: *'For my personal guardian angel...until we meet again',* and underneath the dark scrawl of Alex's autograph: *'Helen—if the halo fits...'*

She hadn't been able to put it down. The element on the kettle had burnt out when she had plugged it in to make a cup of coffee to keep her awake while she read and then forgotten about it. There was no question of nodding off, not until Helen discovered how and why the hero resolved his obsession with the 'Angel' who haunted his wanderings through the chaos of the modern world, and whom he searched endlessly for in his dreams. More than once Helen found herself moved to tears by the writing, so engrossed in the story that she managed to forget that the 'Angel' who intermittently appeared during the hero's darkest hours was a physically accurate picture of herself, right down to the rough, scaly patch of skin on the sole of her left foot, legacy of a childhood burn.

She had finished the last three chapters at the breakfast-table, ignoring the guilty promptings that told her she ought to rush out and pick up a new element for the kettle, so that Anna, when she woke, wouldn't be denied her first fix of coffee for the day. Strangely, despite the fact that she hadn't had any sleep at all, she didn't feel tired, just...slightly foggy, and aware of having made a tactical error. Reading Alex's book was like letting him climb inside her head, now she was carrying something of him around inside her, part of her...

'Wow!' Nicola came back through the curtain, fanning herself. 'There's a guy out there looking at some of your stuff...Canadian, I think, judging from his accent. You want to handle him, or shall I? He's a real dish.' She looked so hopeful that Helen laughed.

'You handle him, I'm an engaged woman.'

And she would do well to remember it. Remember also that she had some explaining to do to her fiancé. She had rung Greg as soon as she had got to work, and arranged for him to come around to the flat for dinner that night. After a slight hesitation Greg had accepted the invitation, with a subdued seriousness that made Helen wonder whether he had come to some conclusions of his own about Alex's behaviour at the nightclub.

'Helen?' Nicola's face tucked around the curtain. 'You're in luck, he wants to meet the author of all those patterns. Come out and swoon...Greg won't mind, so long as you don't run away with the guy, and believe me, once you see him you'll be tempted!'

Helen tucked away her needles and pinned a smile on her face as she went out into the shop. The front window faced north, and for a moment she was dazzled by the sunlight. She blinked.

'Hi, Helen,' said Alex. 'I had no idea you were so talented. These are great pieces of modern art. Have you ever thought of exhibiting?' The 'Canadian' accent was a cosmopolitan purr.

'Alex!' Helen's voice held equal despair and resignation. Was he never going to leave her alone?

'You know each other,' Nicola looked inexpressively disappointed, her reproachful look at Alex met by humorous dark eyes that melted her pique.

'Alex is going to be my brother-in-law,' said Helen, firmly relegating him to where he belonged.

'You're the author? I've read all of your books. Would you give me an autograph?'

'It depends where,' said Alex blandly.

'On my heart, of course,' the jaunty blonde replied. Out of the corner of her eyes she saw Helen's restless movement. So did Alex. He grinned.

'If you have it parcelled up and sent to me, I'm sure I can oblige. Failing that, if you want me to sign a copy of my book, you can give it to Helen and she'll pass it on. Helen and I are going to be seeing quite a lot of each other over the next few weeks.'

'The next few decades, surely,' said Helen quickly, smothering that hint of conspiracy. 'You'll always be welcome to come and stay with Greg and me, Alex, you know that...'

'Oh, I doubt it, in the circumstances,' he murmured, and Helen could see that Nicola was dying to ask, what circumstances?

'Why are you here, Alex?'

'Now, that's a leading question.' Nicola giggled at his hefted eyebrow. 'I came to see you, Helen, about the sweater you promised me. I thought we might discuss it over lunch.'

'I bring a packed lunch to work,' said Helen repressively, stretching the point to cover her fruit and yoghurt. 'And I told you, I'm very busy at the moment.'

'You still have to eat, don't you? I was going to suggest a picnic in the park across the street. I'm sure that Nicola wouldn't mind looking after things here for half an hour or so, would you, Nicola?' His smile was sexy, pleading, rueful and utterly calculated.

'Of course not,' Nicola rushed to assure him, her cheeks pink. 'It's been a little slow here today, anyway. I'll take my lunch later. By all means take off with Helen.'

'Honour forbids me,' said Alex, tongue-in-cheek as he watched Helen try and come up with a valid excuse not to accompany him, one that wouldn't make Nicola more curious than she was already. While he waited he inspected her cool, sleeveless cotton Bali dress with its intriguing crocheted cut-outs. The shop, being small, got quite hot in the summer and, the market atmosphere being very casual, Helen dressed for comfort rather than to impress the customers. Her eye for colour, though, never let her down, and the canary-yellow dress made the most of her golden tan and dark colouring.

Minutes later Helen and Alex were out in the bustle of the market, the unequal battle won without another shot being fired. Reluctant as she was, Helen couldn't help taking an interest in Alex's dilemma over what to buy himself for lunch. Victoria Park Market was unique in the city, a place where fine crafts and expensive clothing vied for space with the cheap and popular. The old brick and wood and corrugated iron factory buildings on the site had been restored to rustic glory to hold a wide variety of shops and stalls, and the bricked inner courtyards of the market were lined with small shops and wagons which sold everything from stained glass to potato peelers. One of the big attractions of the market was the wide variety of foods on offer, and as she trailed Alex from the Mexican counter, to the Italian and Chinese, Helen could feel her own stomach begin to protest the lean pickings awaiting her in the macramé bag slung over her shoulder.

In the end Alex decided on simple elegance over greed. They visited the hot bread shop where he bought a French stick loaf, and then the crammed delicatessen just along from Helen's shop, where Alex selected pâté and cheese and salami, and sent Helen trotting back to get a knife while he paid for his goods.

Meeting up again by the entrance to the market, Helen found Alex carrying, as well as his bulging carrier bag, a soft green and yellow fringed woollen travel blanket under his arm.

When she looked at it askance, Alex shrugged. 'It rained yesterday morning. I thought the grass might still be damp.'

'All that money, for a common or garden *picnic*?' Helen frowned at him. She knew the shop which sold the blankets, and knew she would have thought twice about paying their prices. She also couldn't help being flattered by his impulse. Greg wouldn't have thought of it; on the other hand, Greg wouldn't have suggested a picnic—he'd have taken her to the market restaurant for a 'civilised meal'. Helen struck out across the busy road towards the tree-lined part where a desultory lunch-time cricket match was already going on, not looking back to check whether Alex was following. She shouldn't compare Alex and Greg, they were so dissimilar that comparisons were meaningless and, anyway, Greg would never have taken her for granted the way Alex seemed to... at least he would have *asked* first, and given her the option to refuse without threatening to make a fuss about it.

She was glad of the rug because it was too hot to sit out in the full sun, and under the lacy shade of the oak trees the grass did have a suspicion of dampness. When Alex emptied his carrier bag Helen's eyes widened. There was a cold bottle of white wine, too, and two plastic wineglasses, and succulent, dark golden, marinated chicken wings, and smooth green olives stuffed with scarlet pimentos, and glossy black grapes still bearing a dewy bloom.

'You bought more!' she accused.

'I'm hungry. In case you didn't notice, I didn't eat very well last night.' His eyes drooped to her hungry mouth.

'And you're going to eat all that?' She watched jealously as he broke off a piece of French bread and cut a wedge of beautifully ripe Brie cheese. He brought the cheese up to his lips and Helen's taste-buds tingled in anticipation. How she loved soft, creamy cheeses, and this one looked ripened to perfection.

When Alex opened his mouth, it wasn't to bite, however.

'Tempted?' he teased lazily, grinning knowingly at her as she pretended not to understand the *double entendre*. He switched the cheese from his own lips to hers. 'Go on,' he invited softly. 'Taste. I won't tell.' And he brushed the cut edge of the cheese against her lips so that some of the soft surface beneath the white crust clung and Helen's tongue darted out to savour the creaminess. Alex's eyes darkened, no longer teasing, and Helen froze.

'I think you'd better help yourself.' Alex handed her the knife, and Helen was relieved to have the excuse to look away. Relegating her yoghurt to oblivion, she fell on his offering and, contrary to expectations, enjoyed every bite. Somehow, breaking bread with him made him less of an enemy.

'You look tired,' he said, as she wiped chicken marinade off her sticky fingers with the napkins he had thoughtfully provided. 'Didn't you sleep much after I left you?'

That brought to mind the manner of his leaving. Helen looked over to where a bulky batsman scored an inexpert run, thanks to the fielding side's inertia.

'I read your book.'

'You took it to bed with you?'

Damn it, there it was again—that extraordinary talent of his of making the most innocent statements sound indecent...or was that merely her interpretation?

'I didn't go to bed.'

'Not at all?' He paused, in the midst of emptying the last of the wine into her glass. 'I'm flattered.'

'You don't know what I think of it yet.'

'You liked it.'

'Don't take the words out of my mouth.'

'No, ma'am.' He handed her the glass, his eyes gleaming with laughter at her snappishness.

'I didn't like the ending. It was too...inconclusive.'

'You mean because he never found out whether his Angel was real or not? Where's the romance in *knowing* as opposed to *believing*?'

'It wasn't a romance, it was more of a detective story...or a travelogue through heaven and hell. Of course she wasn't real, she was just a figment of his imagination that he trotted out when he was most in need.'

'You think so?' His smile, she thought, was thoroughly patronising, and she reacted accordingly. Soon they were in heated discussion about the book and its underlying theme of the value of hope as opposed to passive acceptance of one's fate.

Flushed with reckless wine, sated with delicious food, Helen forgot she was talking to the author, the one man who should know, and argued fearlessly for her own point of view.

'You're taking this all rather personally, aren't you, Helen?' Alex said at one point as she knelt over his body, sprawled out on the rug in the masculine splendour of tight, stone-washed jeans and a matching shirt, soft with wear, which at some stage he had unbuttoned to take advantage of the sun, showing a hard, tanned chest lightly sprinkled with soft, red-gold curls.

Helen sat back on her heels again, forgetting what point of view she had been in the process of forcibly expressing. 'I thought that was what you wanted me to do.'

He tucked his arms behind his head, displaying the striations of muscle across his stomach and several faint, silver furrows which could have been scars. Helen's train of thought strayed even further off the path of the conversation.

'So you recognised yourself?'

'Physically,' she allowed him primly. 'The rest was pure embellishment. Was the anguished hero supposed to be you?' She meant it to sound like a jeer, but it came out as merely curious.

'I'm always asked that.' He grinned. 'And I'm always evasive, but you I owe the truth. All my books have an autobiographical element, this one more than most. The incident that inspired it is, as you know, real, and so are my feelings about it. Imagination did the rest. It was tough, because it was an entirely new direction for me and I was terrified of failing...hence the *nom de plume*. I put my heart into that book, Helen, my soul and all my hopes. It was the toughest assignment I've ever tackled, sometimes I wished I was back in the field with bullets whistling around my head, because once you start exploring your own psyche you have to face the ugliness as well as the beauty...the enemy within is a far more terrifying foe than any mere human target. And if you felt the ending was inconclusive, that's because life is inconclusive...one never truly solves the mysteries that haunt one, just as one can never truly know oneself. There has to be something left to search for, or we'd all vegetate in our own smugness.'

'Well, I suppose all that creative torment paid off in the long run. The book made you a very rich man,' she pointed out prosaically, backing away from his seriousness. She already knew more than she wanted to know about Alexander Knight, and he certainly knew too much about her!

'Hinting for a share of the profits, as prime motivator of my talent? Here, these are sweeter.' He held out the decimated bunch of grapes with a provoking smile. She took them without replying and ate them in dignified silence.

'Did any of the passages give you a feeling of *dé jà vu*?'

'No.' She knew where he was leading, but didn't know how to distract him.

'Not even chapter five?'

'Certainly not!' she snapped, feeling a slow blush climb inexorably up from her toes. She began picking up the debris of their picnic.

'That was the one chapter that I didn't have to use my imagination in at all, just my memory... which is excellent, by the way.'

Helen pushed the plastic glasses back into his carrier bag, refusing to look at him. Chapter five had been set in a Hong Kong hotel room, and had contained some of the most erotic writing that Helen had ever come across in her life. Just remembering it made her feel hot and flustered.

A bee buzzed hovered between them, its sultry hum filling the silence. Helen studied it with the dedication of an entomologist. Unfortunately the wretched insect chose to settle on Alex's naked chest, and Helen found herself watching it explore the masculine undulations by now glistening with a light sheen of perspiration. She licked her lips, suddenly feeling parched. She jumped when Alex rolled lazily on to his side, dislodging the wandering bee, and meeting her wide green gaze with a sensuous challenge.

'Did it arouse you, Helen, reading about what we did together?' he murmured softly. 'Did it make you feel all warm and tingly? Did it make your breasts ache and your body feel hollow? Did you enjoy our lovemaking?'

No wonder the bee had sought him out—his tongue dripped honey into the hazy summer air. She wanted to shout out her denial, to utterly reject every shaming word, but she couldn't.

''You're a very effective writer,' she said jerkily.

'Thank you,' he said simply, not challenging now, touched with tender amusement at her evident shyness. She was directing a scowling stare at a group of sparrows that had come to scavenge. 'You're showing an awful lot of interest in birds and bees today, Helen.'

She rounded on him. 'I wish you'd stop talking about it!' she declared, embarrassment replaced by anger, green eyes darkened by storm clouds.

'*It?* You mean sex? There's no need to be embarrassed by your own reactions, Helen. That piece was *supposed* to be highly erotic...I don't think I could have written any other way. The words just flowed out of me as if they had a life of their own, I didn't even have to do a second draft. It made me ache, too, when I wrote it.'

'How could you——?' she choked to a stop, unable to articulate her resentment. But she didn't need to, he knew exactly what she was feeling.

'Use something so private in a book? Writing *Angel in the Dark* was a cathartic experience for me. I *felt* that story so powerfully that I had to get it down on paper. It was like being driven by something outside myself. It also helped me come to terms with my life, to articulate what I wanted for the future, for the best of all futures for mankind. It would have been a betrayal of my feelings not to have included what was for me one of the most powerful physical and emotional experiences of my life...the turning point, if you like. I discovered love, and I was so excited by the discovery that I wanted to share the glory with the whole world!'

Helen stared hopelessly at him, unable to escape the realisation. She knew now why he couldn't let sleeping dogs lie. It wasn't only because of his complex relationship with his brother, it was because Alex *believed* his book. Really believed it. He had projected Helen's image on to the mythical 'Angel' of his intensely coloured imagination, the perfect woman whom he had endowed with all the feminine virtues. In his mind she represented the supreme symbol of desirable womanhood. It was a case of life imitating art with a vengeance!

His laugh at her dawning horror confirmed his madness.

'You think I'm crazy.' His continued empathy was, in the circumstances, unnerving in the extreme. 'Can you blame me? Five years in love with a phantom who suddenly turns up on my own doorstep engaged to the one man in the world I can't trust to love you the way that you should be loved... If it was anyone else, Helen, I just might have let you marry him, *if* I thought he could make you happy.'

'I doubt your ego would consent, even if he was your best friend,' said Helen through her teeth. '*I* trust him. Before—well, he was young, he made a mistake——'

'Mistakes are things that happen inadvertently. Greg knew very well what he was doing and he knew that it was wrong, and, what's more, he thinks the past is important enough to lie about.'

'Lie about? W-what do you mean?'

'I mean, Helen, that it wasn't my *fiancée* that Greg fell in love with, it was my wife. And he didn't just fall in love, he had a full-blooded affair.'

CHAPTER FIVE

'ALICE?' Helen's whisper clogged in her throat. The sluggish air suddenly seemed too thick to breathe.

'Alice.' Alex's dark eyes were wary, his body tense as if he half expected her to physically attack him in angry disbelief. The trouble was that, even in the grip of severe shock, Helen found him all too easy to believe. Alex had made a career out of exposing lies and deceptions, he wouldn't stoop to employing them himself, she knew that instinctively.

'I...' She didn't know what to say. *Alice.* No wonder no one mentioned her without considerable awkwardness, no wonder the family had tread on eggshells around the brothers... it also explained Greg's reticence about his youthful indiscretion, and his deeply uneasy conviction that Alex couldn't possibly have forgiven him.

'No leaping to your fiancé's defence?' Alex's voice was heavily ironic. He sat up, slinging one arm across a bent knee, the other hand dusting crumbs from his outstretched thigh. 'Perhaps you know him better than I thought you did. Perhaps you're content to have him "protect" you from hurt by keeping you in ignorance... to pre-empt your right to make informed decisions about your own life? Of course, in the process he appears in a slightly better light——'

'Alex——'

'Until last night I thought you knew... I thought the "honest relationship" you were so proud of was more than just lip service.'

'I... if I ask him he'll tell me,' Helen defended feebly, but it was too little, too late.

'Of course he will, and in the process he'll manage to share the burden of his guilt with you. Greg is very good at getting other people to shoulder his penance. But will you trust him to tell you the whole of the truth this time, knowing that he's already lied to you once?'

'Would your version of the truth be any more subjective than his?' she asked, trying to sound derisive, but only ending up by appearing uncertain. Alex pounced on that uncertainty.

'Yes, because I've come to terms with what happened. Greg won't let himself. It's not me he really wants forgiveness from, it's himself. I was amazed to hear that he was engaged because I didn't think he'd ever allow himself to be that happy. He doesn't really believe he deserves it.'

'Greg is a very confident, decisive person.'

'In business yes, or when someone else provides the initial impetus.' Helen bit her lip and looked away from his steady gaze, remembering how it had been *she* who had chased Greg, *she* who had set their relationship on the boil.

'Do you want to hear the story, Helen?'

'I owe it to Greg to let him tell me,' she insisted loyally, morbid curiosity clawing at her insides. She ached to know...

'Sometimes being "protected" can hurt more than what you're being protected from, can't it, Helen?' he said gently, and her gaze was irresistibly drawn back to his face, tracing the imprint of fine lines that overlaid a mask of maturity on the golden young boy his had once been. The acuteness of understanding was too much.

'Is that what happened to you?' she faltered, despising herself for giving in to know, not just the truth, but Alex's truth... what he had thought and felt, how he had coped with the enormity of the betrayal.

Some of the tension eased from his body. He smiled, a wry, crooked smile that tugged at her heartstrings. The rolling green playing fields and row of trees under which other lunch-time picnickers lounged disappeared and there was only Alex. Alex the storyteller, Alex the man, with eyes as sweet and dark as bitter chocolate as he drew her into another time, luring her further into an intimacy that was potentially more dangerous than any physical touch.

'When I married Alice we were both young—twenty-one—and full of the crazy optimism of youth. We started on the same newspaper together and shared the same tastes, the same ambitions...I suppose I had visions of us in the future as a famous literary couple.

'But somewhere along the line our ambitions diverged. Alice wasn't really tough enough to be a good reporter, she didn't have the killer instinct and she didn't take rejection or criticism too well, and when you're a reporter you face those two things every day of your working life. So Alice started to drift into the features side of things, while I pursued the hard stuff. I started being offered "glamour" overseas assignments, and the kind of interview opportunities that built up my ego as well as my reputation. We had what I thought was a perfect marriage...Alice was more than content to stay in Auckland, even talking about freelancing so she could start to "build a home", and every time I came home from an out-of-town job she welcomed me with smiles and open arms, and seemed as excited about my prospects as I was. Certainly she never gave me any indication that she was discontented with the amount of time I was spending away...on the contrary, she was positively encouraging.'

For a moment he was silent and Helen forced herself to say, 'Alex, you don't need to tell me this.'

'Yes, I do. I want you to understand why I ran wild for all those years—women, booze, risking my neck for editors who couldn't give a damn about what I went through as long as I met my deadline. I became a thrill-seeker, and once you're locked into that kind of life it can be like an addiction. After a while it lost its gloss and glamour, but by then that kind of reckless, don't-give-a-damn behaviour was expected of me, and the success of the books made everything I did "acceptable" to everyone but me. I refused to trust anyone except myself, after all...' the crooked smile again, without humour '...if you can't trust your own family, who can you trust?'

Helen cleared her throat. She understood all too well the kind of reckless desire to live to the hilt that he was describing, for that was what had sent her on her travels. Facing your own mortality, whether under a surgeon's laser or, as Alex had done, as an observer under fire, certainly put an edge on one's experiences. Her sense of affinity with Alex was getting stronger by the moment.

'How did you find out? Or did you just suspect about Greg and...and your wife?'

'No such luck.' Alex's voice was almost detached as he watched the wicket-keeper, padded up with sweat-shirts belted to his legs, fluke a catch that set up a howl of delight and disbelief from his mates in the field. 'I knew that Greg was keeping an eye on Alice whenever I was away; I didn't realise how closely until I walked in on them one night after a last-minute flight change and caught them in bed...in *my* bed.'

'Oh, Alex...' *Oh, Greg!* How could he?

'I agree, not very discreet,' he said drily, picking up the sympathetic vibrations. 'In fact, after a few years on the rampage, when I finally let myself think about it, I wondered about that...wondered whether perhaps they had *wanted* to be caught, because that would put the onus on me to react, rather than on them to act.

'They'd been in love for months, but they hadn't known how to tell me, hadn't wanted to hurt me, had tried to break it off and couldn't. *I* broke his nose.'

'Greg's?' Helen was horrified, and yet she could imagine Alex, the archetypal male, in a seething fury of pain and frustration, seeking a physical target for his rage and unable to target the woman he loved.

'He didn't even lift a finger to stop me. I would have respected him more if he'd made a fight of it. But Greg isn't like that. He didn't even try and stop Alice leaving. She went back to her parents in Sydney.'

'Did you? I mean, if you loved her...'

'I love the woman I married, but Alice wasn't that woman. She told me before she left that she hated what I was doing, she felt like a useless appendage in my life, and she was as disillusioned with journalism as she was with me——'

'But, she's still *in* journalism.'

Alex looked darkly amused and Helen flushed. She was revealing too much by her curiosity. 'That, my dear Helen, is another story. One thing at a time. Do you understand that the greatest betrayal was not the act, but the lies that concealed it? The lie that Alice lived for *months* because she didn't have the guts to admit that she'd married the wrong man. It made a total mockery of love, theirs and mine. If they'd faced up to it sooner, made *me* face the truth they had so carefully concealed, maybe something could have been salvaged from the mess. Even my parents suspected something was going on, but they didn't say anything either. I felt like a fool. I swore I'd never take another human being at face value. Alice was so...loving. She slept with me out of duty while she was thinking of my brother.'

'Alex, I——' Unthinkingly, she reached out and put her hand on the denim-clad thigh that brushed her knee.

He raised his eyebrows at her. 'Are you going to reassure me, Helen, tell me that my lovemaking is so spectacular that no woman could possibly entertain thoughts of another man? You, who found sex with me spectacularly forgettable.'

Helen removed her hand as if it had been scorched. Here she was, offering him honest compassion, and he was joking about it at her expense! Perhaps he hadn't been as deeply hurt as she had thought his arid words had suggested.

He chuckled as she frowned haughtily at him. 'I told you I was over it, and *I* don't lie. I was young, only twenty-four when the crash came, relatively inexperienced in the harsh ways of the world, although I hardened up fairly quickly after that, and certainly arrogant and egocentric. I thought the world revolved around my ambitions. Finding that I, too, was subject to the whims of fate was rather tough to take. My marriage wasn't perfect just because it suited me. Alice cheated me, cheated Greg and cheated herself, but I wasn't the blameless victim I liked to imagine myself, and of the three of us I think that, in the end, I suffered least. I carried no guilt, you see, I was free to let my ambitions ride me, I became rich and successful on my lost innocence. But still arrogant. I thought I could stop the world and get off when I'd had enough, but I let the emptiness get to me. I cared about great nations, but not about individuals. I was getting stale, afraid that I was losing the ability to *feel* that gave intensity to my writing. Booze gave it back to me temporarily, the "high" that life no longer provided. And then, when I was in danger of suffocating under the weight of years of deliberate emotional disillusionment, I suddenly found something to believe in again. I did the impossible. I rediscovered my innocence...'

The sun had moved. It now fell full on Helen's head, making her feel dizzy. Or was it those hot, dark eyes stripping away her flimsy defences, looking into her mind and heart, at the secrets there, hidden even from herself?

'That's what you gave me that night, Helen,' his voice was soft and slow, enveloping her in its warmth, 'a belief in myself, the knowledge that I could still touch and be touched by emotion. I was a little drunk and very sorry for myself, but you didn't turn away, you didn't judge. You listened to my sorrows, you took me in your arms, and you gave and received joy. You asked nothing and demanded everything. Is it any wonder I fell a little in love with you?' He touched her black head and made a soft sound of amusement. 'Your hair is hot...like hot silk.' He riffled it through his fingers. 'You feel something, too, don't you, Helen? Some physical awareness that transcends the limitation of your memory...something that binds you to me.'

'No...' She shook her head to try and dislodge his hand, but the glossy strands caught between his fingers and gave her hair a sharp tug that brought tears to her eyes.

'Ah, no, love, don't cry.' His mouth hovered dangerously close, and to her horror she wished he wouldn't be so tender and gentle. She wished he would pull her into his arms and overcome the paralysing combination of fear and desire that suddenly flooded her veins.

Heat rose between them, his naked chest an erotic invitation to touch. Helen found herself sinking, sliding into a sensual fog; she felt his skin in hot friction against hers, his breath whispering over breasts as he told her how beautiful and desirable she was; she felt his body hard and heavy between her thighs, moving in a slow, deep, synchronised rhythm.

With an inarticulate cry she scrambled to her feet and stood, swaying, staring at him in hot shame. He hadn't kissed her, had hardly even touched her in fact. It was her own mind that had nearly sent her up in flames.

'What's the matter?' Alex stood up, too, as she tried to mask her turmoil.

'I...I don't like you touching me,' she said harshly.

His concern faded, to be replaced by a gleaming satisfaction. 'Or is it that you liked it too much? What happened, did you remember something about us?'

His undisguised triumph was like a goad. 'You're an attractive man, Alex. I'd have to be dead not to recognise it, but do you know what I find *most* attractive about you? There's a very strong family resemblance. You remind me very much of the man I love! That's the only bond between us. I might have had a past with you . . . but my future is with Greg.'

It was only after she had stormed away that she realised the cruelty of those defensive gibes. She had been defending herself rather than attacking Alex, but he wouldn't see it like that. He would think she was taunting him about his failed marriage. He said he was over it, but she imagined that an intensely masculine man like Alex would find it deeply humiliating to be viewed as a sexual substitute. *'She slept with me out of duty.'* God, what a blow to his pride, to his ego. What love could withstand the burden of being endured as duty? Helen's angry steps had faltered as her conscience prodded her. She ought to go back and apologise, tell Alex that she had only meant to make it clear where her loyalties lay. But she couldn't. She didn't dare. Alex being sexy and sensuous and stimulating was bad enough, Alex vulnerable would be absolutely lethal!

So she left him in the ruins of the picnic and didn't get a lick of work done for the rest of the day, worrying about the coming confrontation with Greg. How should she start . . . with her confession or with his?

As it was, Greg took the decision out of her hands. When he arrived at her apartment that evening the first thing he saw after giving her an abstracted kiss was *Angel in the Dark* on the glass coffee-table.

'I thought you said you hadn't read Alex's book.'

Helen's nerves tautened as he moved to pick it up. If he looked at the dedication page before she had time to

talk to him . . . 'I hadn't. Alex gave that to me last night
and——'

'Last *night*?' Greg stopped dead, his brown eyes narrowing, and Helen had a moment of hot chills at the
likeness. Both brothers, when suspicious, adopted that
brooding, hard-edged look. She was noticing the simi-
larities more and more each day.

'He came around . . . later. He said he thought I ought
to read the book,' she said tentatively, providing herself
with a perfect lead-in. 'You see——'

'He told you, didn't he?' Greg cut her off abruptly,
his voice revealing both anger and relief. 'I *knew* he
wouldn't be able to resist. He told you about Alice, didn't
he?'

'If you knew he was going to tell me, why on earth
didn't you tell me first?' Helen burst out in frustration.
'At least I would have been prepared.'

He turned sharply away from her, increasing her frustration. Alex would have looked her dead in the eye,
forcing her to acknowledge his feelings, gauging hers.

'I was going to. I thought I had more time. I just wasn't
sure how to handle it . . .'

And because of his indecision he was relieved of the
necessity of handling it himself. Helen was reminded
sharply of Alex's version of the events that shattered the
Knight family. Then, too, Greg had had cause to regret
putting off the moment of truth. But she was in no position to throw stones, Helen told herself. She had let
Greg think that Alex had spilled the beans last night,
and she too, was guilty of wanting to 'protect' Greg from
the consequences of her past actions.

'Greg, I——'

He turned back to her, spreading his hands in defeat.
'I knew I'd have to tell you eventually, but I thought I'd
wait and talk to Alex first. I mean, no one but the family
knows the real story behind his divorce . . . it was a mutual
thing based on a separation agreement after . . . after Alice

went back to Australia. I didn't know how Alex would feel if it got out——'

Helen was stung. 'I'm hardly likely to shout it to the world!'

'Oh, I didn't mean that but...' he raked his hand through his neatly trimmed hair, 'I guess I was afraid that it would change us. I—and then Alex was so casual about it, I thought that perhaps I could get away with letting sleeping dogs lie.' His mouth tugged downwards. 'I should have known better. I don't know what triggered him off last night, but suddenly the gloves were off, and Alex packs a lethal punch. All that talk about my finding my own absolution was a pack of lies. Or maybe he meant it at the time, but his feelings got the better of him...'

Now. Now was the time to tell him, to completely clear the air between them. She opened her mouth.

'I suppose you think I'm pretty despicable.'

Helen was reminded of a small boy expecting to be punished: proud and defiant on the outside, crying inside. Helen's best intentions were buried under a sudden avalanche of compassion. Poor Greg—he *hadn't* forgiven himself, and he doubted whether she would, either.

'I think it must have been terrible, for all of you. I'm so sorry, Greg.'

He stood stiffly, taking her apology at face value. 'Does that mean you want to call the wedding off?'

'No! Greg, that's not what I'm sorry about.' Helen was aghast that he could think her so shallow. She went over and put her arms around him. 'I just hate to think of you hurting, that's all. Of course I'm not going to call it off, not over something that happened when I was still a schoolgirl!'

His arms came up and held her tightly, and Helen inhaled the familiar scent of him and felt the steady beat of his heart against her.

Reader Service
FREEPOST
P.O. Box 236
Croydon
Surrey CR9 9EL

PLUS A FREE MYSTERY GIFT

FREE BOOKS CERTIFICATE

YES Please send me my four specially selected Doctor Nurse Romances together with my **free** vase and mystery gift and reserve a Reader Service subscription for me. If I decide to subscribe, I shall receive 6 superb new titles every two months for just £7.50, post and packing **free**. If I decide not to subscribe, I shall write to you within 10 days. The **free** books and gifts will be mine to keep in any case.

I understand that I am under no obligation whatsoever — I can cancel or suspend my subscription at any time simply by writing to you. I am over 18 years of age.

Name: _____ Signature _____
(BLOCK CAPITALS PLEASE)

ADDRESS: _____

_____ Postcode _____

4A9D

POST TODAY!

'Thank you, darling.' His voice was thick with emotion. 'I know Alex must have painted me pretty black——'

'Actually, he said he wasn't a completely blameless victim,' Helen said. She told him Alex's tale, and heard the surprise in his voice as his fierce grip relaxed slightly.

'At the time he claimed that we were just making excuses, but Alice *was* wretchedly lonely, you know. She didn't like the work she was doing, but Alex was so gung-ho about it that he was impossible to talk to. Alice wanted to give up her job and start a family, but Alex wouldn't hear of it, he was having too good a time tearing around the world. Alice used to worry herself sick when he started flitting into trouble spots. I started out as someone to talk to, to keep her spirits up...the rest developed so gradually that by the time we were aware of our feelings it was too late, and once we lost our heads, well...'

'Why didn't she get a divorce earlier, if things were that bad between them?' asked Helen.

'Alice still loved him—not as a husband, of course,' Greg added hurriedly, 'but at first she was torn...she hoped they'd be able to work things out. She'd put Alex first in her life, you see, but in his she'd discovered that she came somewhere down the list, after his job.'

'Are you saying that she didn't think he loved her?'

Greg shrugged awkwardly. 'He loved her, it just wasn't the way Alice wanted to be loved. She wanted a proper home, a husband who was *there* when she needed him, not some by-line in a foreign newspaper. When he was away she was very definite that it was me she wanted, but every time he came back she'd suffer agonies about telling him, wonder if there wasn't something there worth salvaging, after all.'

It sounded a hideous situation, and in Helen's view Alice was largely to blame. It sounded as if she'd wanted to have her cake and eat it, too. Perhaps Greg wouldn't have been so indecisive himself if the woman he'd loved had shown a bit more spunk. Helen's illness had made her very aware of the perils of letting life drift by you. If Helen saw something she wanted, she went for it. In the last five years she had met all her major goals, and regularly set new ones for herself. Regrets were more likely to visit those who had never even tried for their dreams than for those who had reached for the stars and fallen short.

Greg echoed her thoughts. 'Thank God you're not like that. I guess I was pretty immature in those days and a bit jealous of Alex. Alice . . . well . . . that was obviously never meant to be, right from the start. But I don't know what I'd do if I lost you, Helen. You've brightened up my life and made me realise what I was missing . . . love, a home, kids. When Alex sent that acceptance back and then turned up out of the blue, I suppose all the old insecurities came rushing back. But he can only break us up if we let him, and we're not going to do that, are we, darling?'

'No.' Helen accepted his fierce embrace, using it to try and smother her dismay. Brave words, but she had heard the hollow ring behind them. Fleetingly she was irritated by his obvious vulnerability, and then she was ashamed of herself. It wasn't fair to resent Greg for the very sensitivity that was so much a part of the man she had fallen in love with. And it was pure selfishness to resent it now, just because she had wanted to clear her own conscience. Procrastination was an anathema to her and, in the present circumstances, unpleasantly ironic, but Helen couldn't bring herself to aim yet another blow at Greg's already crippled self-esteem. She would take it step by step, work gently around to the subject of her misty past.

She wasn't going to lose Greg. She wasn't going to allow anything to wreck his second chance at love.

Alexander Knight was a ghost that she had every intention of laying permanently to rest, but in her own way, in her own time.

Helen was nobody's angel, and it was about time Alex realised it, even if it meant ramming the fact down his handsome throat!

CHAPTER SIX

'TAKE my advice,' Greg's cousin said. 'Call it off now, before it's too late. You've still got ten days. I can't believe that he asked you to give up your business and stay home and have his babies. I thought Greg was *civilised*!'

Helen was beginning to be sorry that she had teased Josephine. It was just that the girl, two years into law at university, was so aggravatingly serious about her newly acquired feminist ideals. When she had cornered Helen and started to interrogate her about why she wanted to get married and give up everything that she had worked for just for the sake of out-dated convention, Helen had known that it was pointless to argue. Only, her humour had rebounded on her, and for the past fifteen minutes she'd had to listen to an earnest lecture on the rights and responsibilities of today's women.

In fact Helen had come in for quite a few lectures, one way and the other, today. The welcome-home party for Alex had grown from a few close relatives to the whole Knight clan, in all their myriad forms. Many of them Helen herself had not been expected to meet until the wedding, and some of those seemed to bear a friendly grudge that she and Greg hadn't had a large engagement party. Knight family gatherings, it was apparent, were considered a right rather than a privilege on such occasions. She sensed that she and Greg had only been forgiven because their courtship had been so swift, but that meant putting up with sharp looks at the drop-waisted dress that she had made the mistake of wearing.

'He might act like a liberated male, but he's a caveman in private,' said Helen, and Josephine was halted in full flight, her Knight-brown eyes rounding as she realised she had been taken for a prolonged ride.

'Helen——' she began severely, then something beyond Helen's shoulder caught her eye. She grinned maliciously and raised her voice. 'Hello, Aunt Mary, Helen's just here, dying to have a word with you.'

Helen whipped around, but it was too late. The straw hat bedecked with flowers was bobbing towards them and Aunt Mary, once having latched on a target, had all the deadly accuracy of a heat-seeking missile.

'Oh, I think I hear my mother calling,' said Josephine with a very sweet, very feminine, very un-Josephine smile as she backed away. 'Now, you be nice to Aunt Mary, Helen. You and she will have loads to talk about, seeing as you're so closely related in your personal philosophies!'

Helen buried her rueful smile in a hefty swig of wine. Aunt Mary was really Great-Aunt Mary, the oldest surviving member of the Knight family and thus endowed with an almost mystical ability to cause maximum embarrassment in the shortest time. 'The privilege of age', she called her habit of making outrageous remarks. Although they hadn't met, Helen had heard enough about her to avoid actively promoting an introduction.

'You been avoiding me, girl? Got something to hide, have you?' were the old lady's first words, spoken in a surprisingly spritely voice for a ninety-two-year-old.

'No, no, of course not,' Helen stuttered, aware of smiles around them. When you weren't the target, Aunt Mary could be good entertainment. She also quite obviously relied on her years to duck the rules of common courtesy. 'I thought it was the other way around. Who's the good-looking guy with you?'

There was a startled silence, then Aunt Mary's bleached blue eyes crinkled up and she gave a cackling laugh. 'Got your eye on him, have you? He boards with me. He's my minder.' Helen had noticed a few curious looks when the old lady had made her appearance with a very handsome teenager in tow. The whisper was that he was a third cousin by marriage, up from the country to attend an apprenticeship course at a technology institute.

'Of course he is, Aunt Mary,' said Helen in a sceptical voice. It worked. There was another cackle.

'I like you, girl. None of that smarmy "yes, ma'am" stuff. I like a woman who stands up for herself. Not too much, mind. No man likes a shrew.'

'Yes, ma'am,' said Helen meekly. She sipped her wine decorously this time, thankful that she had the old lady's measure. But she relaxed too soon.

'Never been married myself. Fiancé died at Gallipoli. No one else ever matched up. Don't believe in marrying just for the sake of it. What are you marrying for?'

'I love him, Aunt Mary.'

'Not pregnant, are you?' In the clear evening air of the Knights' carefully tended orchard where everyone had gathered for a barbecue, Mary Knight's piercing demand brought a momentary lull in conversation. Helen could have sunk through the ground. She wished Greg would come and rescue her, but last time she had seen him he had been in the kitchen with some of his male cousins, being pestered about the date and location of his bachelor party.

'No,' she gritted in an undertone.

'No?' Aunt Mary echoed loudly. 'Good, good, just wanted to get that settled.' One crêpey eyelid drooped in a wink, and she continued at a more normal level. 'That'll shut the gossips up. This family is a terrible one for rumours. Never say anything to your face, but yabber like monkeys behind your back.'

'Perhaps I should have had it engraved on the invitations: "This is not a shotgun marriage",' said Helen tartly, unable to appreciate the old lady's tactics.

'Now, don't you get huffy with me, young lady. Your own fault, you know. No smoke without fire. A couple in such a rush as you two have to raise some questions in people's minds.'

'And you were delegated to ask them? You disappoint me, Aunt Mary, I was told you had a mind of your own.'

A rusty chuckle. 'That was no compliment, my girl. No, I see the fire all right. I see you watching him and him watching you. I may be old, but I'm not dead. My Eric and I, we knew each other from babyhood, we grew into loving each other. But I know it happens the other way. I know sometimes you're not looking where you're going and you trip up and, hey, you fall and there ain't no way out. That's the way I see it with you and Alex.'

The glass slipped in Helen's hands. 'Greg, you mean Greg, Aunt Mary.'

'Do I?' The cunning old eyes were all innocence. Helen felt her guilt written in letters of fire ten feet high. *Had* she been watching Alex? If she had, it had only been to avoid him. She hadn't seen him since their lunch together, and Greg had firmly vetoed any more double-dates, his animosity towards his brother for interfering restrained only for his parents' sake.

'It's Greg I'm going to marry, Aunt Mary. I've only just met Alex,' she said sharply.

'Course, Alice was all wrong for Alex. No gumption... not then, anyway. Brains, but not smart. You strike me as a pretty smart girl. Like to travel too, don't you? Like *change*. Not Greg. If he hadn't messed up he would have been quite happy to sit back and vegetate in domesticity. Look at it that way, Alice did them both a favour by running out. Lit a fire under them. By the looks of them it's still burning. Course, Alex has always been good at fanning flames. Makes a body wonder how come he hasn't burnt out by now, but here he is, live as life, still striking sparks. You flammable, girl?'

'I'm not in the market for an arsonist.' Helen's nerves were at snapping point, and she was thankful that Nicholas had called out that the steaks were ready, and most of the eavesdroppers in the vicinity had wandered over to the groaning trestle-tables set out under the greening trees. She hated to think of the rumours that *this* crazed conversation could start. 'I happen to be perfectly happy at the thought of domesticity.'

'Cool down, girl, only asking,' the wretched old woman chuckled. 'Does Greg know you've got a temper? He doesn't like arguments, you know. If you've got a temper, you'd be better off with Alex. He enjoys a good fight . . . lots of action in *his* life. Don't you go making Alice's mistake, missy. Don't you go messing about those boys. Can't stand a woman who can't make up her mind.'

'Aunt Mary——' Helen began furiously. The old lady was ten times worse than she had been warned she was. Only she found she was chewing on thin air. Aunt Mary had spied another juicy victim, a niece who had just divorced her husband of twenty-five years.

'Perspicacious old duck. I always thought she would have made a hell of a reporter.'

'Senile, you mean.' Helen glared after the bobbing hat, partly in frustration at being denied a cutting reply, partly to control herself before turning reluctantly to look at Alex. 'How long have you been standing there?'

'Long enough to hear you lie through your teeth. Domesticity, my eye. That won't make you happy. You may want a husband and family, Helen, but you need a hell of a lot more besides.'

'How long have you been writing your Dear Abby column, Alex?' she sniped sarcastically, and he grinned at her, his teeth white and even against the tan that had deepened in the short while he had been in New Zealand.

In a loose white T-shirt and pale blue shorts that revealed long, well-muscled legs that put Tom Selleck's to shame, Alex was the most casually dressed man present. And the most blatantly sexy. Sunlight suited him, gilding his masculinity, making Helen resent him even more.

'The voice of experience, my dear. I know how exquisitely you respond to...stimulation.'

Helen stiffened. 'If you dare say one thing to Greg, to anyone——'

'Coward,' he said softly. 'You haven't told him yet, have you? You let him weep on *your* shoulder. Don't you think he's strong enough to take it?'

'The situation is very different...and you aren't helping it, either.' Not the way he kept flinging unpalatable truths in her face.

'You can't trust his love, that's the problem here, Helen. I may have created the conflict, but I don't *have* to do any more stirring. You and Greg are supplying all the agitation. I'm just holding a watching brief.'

'Can I rely on that?' she snapped.

He put a flat hand over his chest. 'Cross my heart.'

'I didn't know you had one.'

'Well, I must admit, it's not in my immediate possession...' He gave her a warm, liquid look that melted in her veins.

'Damn you!' She could feel herself flush, and only hoped that everyone would put it down to sun.

'Darling?' It was with a shock that she felt Greg's arm slide around her waist and pull her possessively against her side. 'Haven't you got anything to eat yet? Come on over or you'll miss out. This family is a pack of scavengers.'

Helen had the feeling he wasn't referring to the crowd around the white trestle-tables, groaning with food, that had been erected beneath the greening trees.

''We' were just having an innocent conversation, Greg,' said Alex with a mocking smile.

Helen felt Greg's fingers tense on her hip. 'Helen didn't look as if she was enjoying it.'

'It's all right, Greg,' Helen hastened to tell him. 'Alex was just being his usual....' She sought for the right word.

'Provocative?' Alex supplied in a sultry voice that was a provocation in itself.

'I was going to say *obnoxious* self,' said Helen firmly. With difficulty she turned Greg's antagonistic body aside with her own. 'Actually, I *am* starving. Let's go and see if your father has a steak that's small enough for me.'

After that it seemed every time she turned Alex was at her shoulder, and yet apparently only by coincidence, for he was too busy entertaining his relatives to pay any more unwelcome attention to his brother and the woman he had clamped to his side. Helen found Greg's protectiveness both touching and slightly claustrophobic. God, she would be relieved when the wedding was over and they could all relax. *But would they?* a small voice whispered. Was she expecting too much to think that marriage would magically smooth over all the little rough spots that the last couple of weeks had revealed in their hitherto smooth relationship? Unfortunately Greg was leaving on an unexpected three-day trip to Bangkok the next day, to patch up an important export deal that had fallen through at the last moment, and Helen was acutely aware of time slipping inexorably by. Greg would be back in time for the wedding rehearsal, but his absence put a spoke in Helen's plan to quietly prepare him for the shock that was coming. It wasn't that she was a coward, she denied Alex's accusation to herself, but she wanted to be as certain as she could be that Greg felt secure in her forgiveness before she sought his. That was prudence, not cowardice.

The sky blushed as evening drew her skirts in. Although it was still quite light, someone lit the torches scattered around the orchard and, while the youngest members of the clan darted in and out of the trees in frantic games of hide and seek, the elders drifted inside for tea and coffee and gossip. Teenagers turned on a portable stereo and marked out the closely mown strip of grass by the barbecue as their personal property, while those in their twenties and thirties clustered around the outdoor bar to catch up on each other's lives since the last family occasion, the christening of a child who now lay fatly asleep in a pushchair, oblivious to the noise and activity around her.

Alex, naturally, was the main focus of interest. Plied with questions, he spoke lightly of his years of adventuring, of the famous people he had met.

It wasn't boasting, and yet Helen couldn't help but agree when a disgruntled Greg muttered 'show off' in her ear. It was a thriller-writer talking, not the complex man who had produced *Angel in the Dark* and the more recent novels, nor the whimsical one who claimed, with misguided sincerity, to have refound innocence of heart. This Alex was as innocent as the devil. As he related the tale of a distinguished stage actress of venerable years and her nude frolic with a Third World leader in the fountain of a French château, Helen felt a vague sense of disappointment. So what if he enjoyed his celebrity status? One couldn't say that he hadn't earned it.

A little later, when Greg's restlessness got the better of him, Helen joined him in a stroll among the trees. She couldn't help feeling that when Greg stopped, just beyond the circle of avid listeners, to kiss her long and thoroughly, it was more a case of thumbing his nose at his brother than being overcome with desire. When he finally let her go and she looked back over her shoulder, Alex, laughing at a joke, was watching them and his eyes were not amused.

Hot words leapt to Helen's lips, but she held them in. She couldn't accuse Greg of trying to annoy his brother without revealing that she herself was acutely aware of

Alex's every move. A wave of anger at her helplessness swept over her. How she hated the trapped feeling that the situation had generated; it reminded her of her months of illness, the terrible sensation of an enemy that she had no weapons against, burgeoning within.

They didn't get very far along the rows of apple, plum, pear and peach trees before they were ambushed by youngsters, bored with their games, and soon Greg was organising two teams for a scavenger hunt.

Helen was amused at how quickly Greg's mood changed. She was forgotten as he handed out hastily written lists and explained the rules...and the prize. For a bachelor Greg got on extremely well with children. He seemed to have a genuine interest in their thoughts and deeds, and they responded warmly. He would make an excellent father and even had a fondness for babies that most men lacked. Helen would have liked to wait a little while before having children, but she knew that Greg would rather start a family straight away and she wasn't about to tempt fate by denying him. She could always work from home and travel with the baby. At least she knew that Greg would take a keen interest in sharing the parenting!

After helping a few of the children find a particularly shaped leaf, Helen wandered off by herself towards the creek that ran diagonally across the bottom of the property. She loved company, but sometimes, especially lately, she felt the need to be alone with her thoughts.

The Knights had the best of both worlds here, she thought a trifle enviously: all the conveniences of suburbia on a section big enough to have a feeling of country about it. Luckily Nicholas Knight was extremely fit and had no trouble looking after the extensive grounds, and when it got too much for him Greg intended to pay for a gardener and handyman rather than suggesting his parents wrench themselves away from the place where they had lived for their entire married life. Dear Greg.

If only he could get over his inferiority complex about his brother, he would be the perfect man. But then, who in this world was perfect?

'Angel?'

Helen gave a small shriek as a figure detached itself from the shadow of a tree. Down here, where there were no torches and the ground rose on a steady plane towards the house, it was almost dark.

'Sorry. Did I frighten you?'

'Constantly.' The word fell out before she could stop it and her heart thudded uncomfortably. Now he would say something mocking or suggestive.

'I came down to look at the creek. Greg and I used to spend hours down here when we were kids, damming it and having model raft races, and "accidentally" falling in. It was the big draw of the neighbourhood. Now I see several pools around, I suppose a creek is old hat.'

'Mud and running water is never old hat,' said Helen, her heart slowing. 'But it must have been a bit of a worry for your mother.'

She saw the dim flash of teeth. 'We were well within screaming distance and, believe me, there were a few screams. No, it was the mud that used to drive Mum crazy. And when we grew out of mud-fights we took up rugby. What Mum wouldn't have done for an automatic washing machine and enzyme detergents in those days.'

'Mmm, I know what you mean.' Helen remembered her own grubby childhood.

'Do you, China girl? You look so sweet and feminine, I can't believe that your mother didn't dress you in frills and ribbons and give you pretty dolls to have tea parties with rather than let you get involved in rough and tumble games.'

Helen burst out laughing. She knew from his tone of voice that he was teasing, but he was curious, too. 'You couldn't be more wrong. My parents had a share-milking business on a dairy farm. Susan and I grew up in gumboots and patches. We only had one "going out" dress each. We each had a pig of our own to raise, and nothing was more fun than hopping in the pen with them and playing tag. And mud-pies were a speciality of the house at our tea parties!'

'You were a tomboy?' Alex bent to pick up a twig and throw it into the dark, swirling water at their feet. Automatically Helen did the same.

'I was a child...certainly no angel,' she said pointedly. 'There wasn't a lot of money around, so we had to make our own entertainment. But we had a ton of love and there's a lot of security in living close to the land, even if it isn't your own private piece.'

'You sound like a real country girl at heart. Are you happy living in the city?'

'I wouldn't be here if I wasn't. The country was a great place to grow up in, but I was already in Auckland, training at secretarial college, when my parents were killed, and I didn't feel there was anything to go back for. Besides, I was ready for new experiences.'

'You were going to be a secretary?'

'Ha!' She snorted as his stick sank and hers forged out of sight around the curve of the creek. 'I didn't have any ambition at all really, so it seemed to be a safe bet. Afterwards...I wasn't interested in safe bets, I learned to make the most of every opportunity, and all the soothing knitting that the hospital psychologist recommended I do was one of them. It gave me the kind of freedom that office work could never have done. I didn't have to stay in one place to save up the money to do what I wanted to do, I could earn my way as I went.'

His questions flowed naturally from her remarks, and in turn the answers came with remarkable ease. It was only when her throat began to feel dry that Helen realised how much she had been talking, even about the dark days that she usually glossed over, the constant fear, the strain of putting on a brave face to her friends, the realisation of the intrinsic, inevitable loneliness of the human spirit, the constant round of debilitating tests and treatment in a ward where a vacant bed meant another new friend lost, another battle fallen to the foe...

'Is it my imagination, or have I just been skilfully interviewed?' she asked drily. 'You're a very subtle questioner—no wonder you get all those scoops. Shouldn't you have shown me your Press pass first, or am I just an entertaining tale to tell your friends?'

'Strictly off the record.' She thought he was going to ignore her dart. 'And I suppose you're referring to that little session back there that so bored you and Greg. I was only telling them what they wanted to hear, and none of it was a secret, they could have read the details in any newspaper at the time. I only added a bit of personal colour. Do you really think that they'd be interested in the *real* story of my life? Didn't you notice the scandalous bits were all over five years old? My life at the moment is almost monkish...ten hours a day sitting in front of a typewriter, talking to myself.'

'Every day?' Helen raised her eyebrows in the dimness to show him she was not impressed, although secretly she was curious about the working habits of a famous author.

'Well, I did say *almost*,' he admitted in amusement. 'I have to let off steam sometimes. It's difficult to sustain that kind of creative intensity for months on end if you don't take nights off. You must find yourself that you need regular...er...stimulation to produce of your best...to spark off...'

Helen's eyebrows lowered sharply.

'Not that kind of stimulation, Helen,' he told her blandly. 'I'm referring to the mental kind. Intellectual input that can only come from other minds. Physically speaking, I'm as chaste as you are.'

Dangerous ground. Helen at once retreated. 'If it's so difficult, why do you do it?'

'Because I can't *not*. Because the end result gives me enormous emotional satisfaction. To me, it's a great luxury to be able to devote long stretches of my time writing on one theme. I spent years writing out of a suitcase, half the time never seeing what I'd written in print because I was already off chasing the next story. And those wham-bam-thank-you-ma'am thrillers were done the same way, until they became almost parodies of themselves…written in a dozen different hotel rooms, drunk or sober, it didn't seem to make much difference to the end product. Now I plan my projects in terms of months rather than days, I do my research and then I lay it out around me and sit down and don't get up again until *I* want to. And I'm proud of what I write. I'd lost that pride in myself, buried it in cynicism. It took a glimpse of heaven to persuade me it was worth getting back.'

'Alex——' Helen shied at the deepening of his voice, and this time the dangerous ground was right beneath her feet, the soft clay of the creek bank. She slipped, and Alex's hand shot out with lightning speed to catch her before her feet touched the water, hauling on her forearm as his other hand scooped around her waist, his body straining as he dipped to take her weight. The backward momentum of his pull carried them through the lacy veil of a weeping willow, the fronds falling back into place behind them so that they were suddenly enclosed in a hushed and private world of green-filtered dimness.

'Are you all right?'

Not while he was holding her. His touch was light, but it held her more securely than chains. She was afraid to move, afraid of triggering the tension that had swept through his hard body when she had bumped against him.

'Helen…' The sensuous yearning he made of her name unlocked her frozen tongue.

'Alex, I'm very flattered that you should consider me as the inspiration for a very fine book, but that's as far as it can go. I'm not your "Angel". Even if I wanted to be, I couldn't live up to the character that you created in your own mind. If you're so sure I'm the "Angel" you've put up on that ridiculously high pedestal, why are you trying so damned hard to shake me off?' All her frustration was in the quiet cry.

'Because I love you.'

'Even if that were true, so what?' She was furious with him for sounding as if he truly believed it. 'That's your problem, not mine. We were two ships that passed in the night——'

'That *docked* in the night,' he corrected her with grim amusement that made her grind her teeth. It was definitely time for her to put her foot down, and suddenly she knew where to place it for maximum effect.

'—and I refuse to be made accountable for something that I don't even remember happening. That's why I'm not going to tell Greg.'

There was a momentary stunned silence. 'What did you just say?' Alex asked, in a voice full of quiet menace. Helen's eyes strained in the dimness to read the expression on his face, but it was closed to her. She licked her lips. Had she misjudged him, after all?

'I'll tell him there was a man—once—but that's all. I won't tell him who it was, and I know he won't ask. Because he knows it isn't important.'

Alex's hand closed savagely on her arm. 'What makes you so sure *I* won't tell him?'

'Because I don't believe you want to hurt him, any more than I do. I don't believe that a man who talks and writes the way you do could be so callous. I'm calling your bluff, Alex.'

She expected him to rage, she expected him to continue his bluff. She was thoroughly disconcerted when he made a soft sound of disbelief.

'You trust me that much?'

'I . . . yes.'

'Interesting. You trust *me* with your secrets, but not the man you claim to love.'

'I . . . you can't compare the way I feel about Greg with——'

'The way you feel about me?' he asked huskily, the fingers that had been digging into the soft flesh of her arm now stroking over the tingling skin. 'I know. That's because there's no convenient label to put on your feelings about me. You've already used the only one that fits—for Greg. Why do you find it so difficult to believe that *I* fell so hard and so swiftly in love with you, and so easy to believe Greg?'

He didn't ask easy questions, but then he specialised in complexity. 'Because it was mutual, that's why. You're not in love with me, Alex, you're just feeling possessive because I'm part of the book you're so proud of. You're in love with an idea!'

'Then how do you explain your attraction to *me*? And don't insult me by telling me it's my likeness to Greg.'

'But it's true.'

'Yes, but it works both ways. Greg looks like *me*. Hasn't it yet occurred to you why you were so instantly and deeply attracted to Greg? Because, subconsciously, he evoked the emotions you felt when you were with *me*!'

She stared at him, stunned by the memory of the first time Greg had kissed her. She told him that being in his arms was like 'coming home'. They had even teased each other about it, speculating that they had been lovers in a previous existence.

'Absolute rubbish!' she snapped, pulling away from his heated body, turning from the picture of thinly veiled masculinity he presented, his white T-shirt almost ghostly in the dusk, his sensual appeal almost physical in its intensity.

But he had seen the flicker in her quick hostility, and when he followed her through the curtain of willow his hard mouth was curved with satisfaction that increased when he watched Helen's angry figure breast the top of the rise and the last rays of sunset glanced darkly off her head, making it look as though she wore a corona of red-gold...or a halo.

Helen almost walked slap-bang into Greg, coming to look for her.

'Where have you been?' His jaw jutted sullenly. 'With *him*?'

Helen felt a slow tingle in the bottom of her spine as Alex sauntered up beside her, his hands in his pockets stretching his shorts almost indecently tight across the tops of his hair-roughened thighs.

'We were just talking,' she said hurriedly.

'What about?'

Helen resented his sharp demand, even though she understood what provoked it. 'Nothing, really...our childhoods, his books...'

'Is that all?'

Helen stiffened, but it was Alex who spoke, in an amused drawl. 'Why the Spanish Inquisition? Do you think Helen is the type to kiss and tell?'

Helen forgot herself so far as to snap, 'No, but he can be sure you are!'

'What the hell does that mean?' Greg's suspicion deepened, and to her alarm Helen noticed his fists balled at his side.

'Nothing.' Alex shrugged. 'I hardly even touched her——'

He didn't get time to finish. With a low roar Greg was on him, tumbling them both to the ground. Helen was frozen to the spot as the brothers rolled and grappled and cursed, muscles bulging in all too real combat. Both men were roughly the same size, but Greg was softer, less conditioned, and he looked faintly absurd in his elegant trousers and designer shirt acting out the macho ethic with someone who looked dangerously happy to oblige. Thank goodness they had rolled a little way back down the incline, out of sight of the noisy revellers by the house.

'Greg! Alex! Stop it, both of you!' Her protests were useless, they were deaf and blind to everything but their private little war. She didn't matter at all, she realised, and a cleansing fury swept through her. If the creek had been at hand she would have doused them with water like fighting tomcats, but all there was was a bucket of tiny hard green fruit, windfalls, a mist of fruit-flies attesting to their damaged condition. A muffled crunch drove Helen into action. She picked up the bucket and threw the contents as hard as she could at the tussling men. There were fresh curses as the fruit bounced off their targets, and two pairs of almost identical brown eyes glared up at her. They both looked furious, but at least they had stopped fighting.

'What did you do that for?' Greg growled at her.

'Get up!' When they didn't move, Greg's hand still fisted in Alex's T-shirt, Alex half on top of him, tilting to look over his shoulder at Helen, she repeated. 'Get up!' Neither man had ever heard her use that tone of voice before. Helen couldn't remember hearing it herself, it was icily frozen, carrying the threat of blue murder.

Slowly the two men disentangled themselves and got stiffly to their feet, watching Helen warily. For a brief moment she had an almost irresistible urge to laugh. Broad-shouldered, towering over her, they managed to look like two chastened little boys. She bit her lip and willed herself not to soften.

'I am not a bone to be fought over. I don't happen to find it exciting to watch your macho posturings,' she told them coldly. 'And I refuse to be the excuse for you to carry your private little war to ridiculous extremes. Look at yourselves!' Hands on hips, a scornful toss of her head indicated their rumpled, grass-stained clothes and reddened faces. 'What if one of the children had seen you? What sort of example is that to set? What if your *mother* got to hear? You know how much she's depending on this wedding bringing the family together, not splitting it further apart. Or are you both so blinded by your own grievances that you don't *care* about the people who love you? And you, Alexander.' She took a step forward, bristling with her anger, and poked a finger at his chest, causing him to wince. 'I thought you'd seen enough fighting. The peace-monger, isn't that what the Press call you these days? Settling your arguments with your *fists*? And you can take that smirk off your face, Greg.' She swung around on her fiancé, her green eyes spitting temper. 'You were spoiling for a fight even *before* you saw us, *and* you threw the first punch. You are *supposed* to be mature adults, and adults, at least those who are half-way intelligent, don't settle their differences with violence. Now, you'd better go around the side and get tidied up before anyone else sees you. But before you go——' She stopped them with an imperious hand as they turned, slightly dazed by her tempestuous tirade, to obey. 'Before you go, I want you to shake hands.'

Incredulous brown eyes suddenly mirrored sullen looks.

'*Do it!*' Her blistering order was hesitantly obeyed, Alex holding his hand slowly out and Greg reluctantly taking it in a brief shake that barely passed as contact.

For a moment tension flickered around the small group, and then Greg shifted sheepishly, brushing ineffectually at the brown stain a decomposing plum had left on his expensive cream shirt.

'Can we go now?'

Helen frowned at him, suspicious of his meek tone.

'Are we still allowed to have some supper?' asked Alex, equally meek.

Helen glared at them. So... they thought it was funny now! 'Oh, just go away, both of you!'

She watched them skirt the trees at the side of the house, noting the stiffness of their dirt- and grass-stained backs. Alex was limping slightly and Greg was rubbing his arm. Still, at least they were walking together, and perhaps that glimmer of humour had been a good thing, even though it had infuriated her after the shock of the physical confrontation.

Mentally she dusted off her hands. After two weeks of wobbling along an emotional tightrope, permanently off balance, she had found her feet again, regained her ability to think and act decisively, her self-confidence.

For the first time, she felt that things might turn out all right, after all!

CHAPTER SEVEN

'Wow, Helen, I've never had such a good time in my life. You ought to get married more often!' Nicola West laughed, her blonde hair curling fashionably around her small face as she poured herself another glass of wine.

'Certainly the most exciting bridal shower I've ever been to,' another of Helen's friends grinned.

'All I can say is I'm glad that I didn't invite Aunt Mary,' said Greg's mother, her face still pink with laughter and embarrassment.

'Well, we didn't realise that you were coming, Mrs K,' said Anna as she came out of the kitchen of the small apartment, bearing fresh cups of tea and coffee on a tray to offer the chattering group of women, 'or we would have been more circumspect...either that or we would have asked you to chip in for the *full* performance.' She waggled her eyebrows wickedly and Helen giggled. Her girlfriends had all chipped in to hire a male stripper to crash the Saturday afternoon tea party, but in the interests of economy they had settled for the 'cheap' version, in which the young man in question had only peeled down to bikini briefs. Hannah, who had arrived unexpectedly with her sister, had caused a momentary panic, but after a hurried conference in whispers it was decided that she would be a good sport about it. Helen had a sneaking suspicion that Hannah had been less embarrassed and more intrigued than she let on. It was Helen, focus of the stripper's attention and blushing recipient of his cast-off clothing, who had been the most flustered.

'Hey, guess what...he forgot something!' Nicola dangled a small leather loincloth from dainty fingers, the last garment that had been cast off. 'You're gonna have fun returning this, Helen. He's sure to think you hid it on purpose just to see him again. Better make sure it's before D-Day, though.'

'You hired him, you return it,' Helen told her amid laughter.

'Return? Hell, I might wear it myself.' Nicola held it up in front of her and pranced around the room, winding through the presents that littered the floor among their discarded wrappings. As well as the small kitchen items her friends had given her, larger wedding presents had begun to arrive, and Helen was feeling rather overwhelmed with people's generosity. At this moment she was seeing the whole world through a rosy glow.

'Well, I suppose Ida and I should be on our way,' Hannah said reluctantly when they had finished their tea. 'You put on a lovely spread, girls, and Nicholas is just about going to burst a blood vessel when he hears what we've been up to.'

'Don't you go making comparisons, Mrs Knight,' said Nicola. 'This shower was to speed a marriage, not a divorce.'

'He was a very nicely built young man,' Hannah said primly. 'But I'll take my Nicholas any day. Bulging biceps are no match for experience. Nicholas was quite a lad in his day, you know. *Quite* a lad.' She winked at Helen who, seeing Ida's disapproval, was trying hard to look neutral.

'Come along, Hannah,' her sister said, taking her arm and firmly drawing her towards the door. 'I think you've had one too many glasses of wine. You, too, Melissa.'

Ida's married daughter pulled a face as she gave Helen a quick farewell kiss. 'Mum's just miffed because I didn't have a stripper at *my* shower,' she whispered. 'Maybe I should hire one for her next bridge club meeting. Wouldn't that be a gas!'

Several others took their leave, and soon there were only half a dozen guests left telling tipsy jokes and swapping stories about their men-troubles. When the doorbell rang Helen was sent to answer it, loincloth in hand.

'Make sure he gives you a kiss for it!' Anna laughed.

But it wasn't the cheeky young dancer standing outside the door. It was Alex, relaxing and smiling in jeans and a fluorescent T-shirt that made her eyes wince. He was carrying a brown paper bag and a gift-wrapped parcel.

He didn't say anything, merely tilting an eyebrow at her, and Helen felt her shock die into a seething resentment. She hadn't seen him since the day of the Knights' party, but even so he hadn't left her alone. His taunt about the source of her feelings for Greg haunted her with relentless constancy, and at night, in defenceless sleep, she was visited by disturbingly erotic dreams of a faceless lover whom she didn't dare try to identify. The uneasy truce established between the brothers after their fight was another source of worry. Of course Helen had wanted them to settle their differences, but not in a way that made her feel inexplicably excluded... Greg having refused to tell her what had passed between the two men while they had been inside cleaning up. Whatever it was, they had come out smiling and joking as if all problems were resolved, while Helen's loomed larger than ever.

'What are you doing here, Alex?' The thick, dark arch of her eyebrows snapped together as he looked her over in a pointed manner that told her she had been staring. She was glad that she was wearing one of her prettiest dresses, a strapless yellow cotton that flattered her curves and showed lots of creamy skin, and annoyed that she should care.

'I heard you were having a party.'

'Females only,' she confirmed unsmilingly. 'You have to wait for Greg's bachelor party, presuming you're *invited*.' She started to close the door on that snidery, but some expensive Italian leather got in the way. 'Take your foot out of the door, Alex.'

'Don't you want my present?' He raised his voice plaintively. 'I bought a couple of bottles of champagne, too, to toast your happiness.'

'Which you happen to be doing your best to try and destroy,' hissed Helen, trying to kick his foot out of the way so that she could slam the door on temptation.

'Did I hear someone say champagne?' Anna came up behind Helen. 'Who is that out there?'

'An encyclopaedia salesman,' snapped Helen.

'Bearing champagne? It must be a big seller,' grinned Anna. 'What's he selling, an encyclopaedia of sex? Is he offering demonstrations?'

'Only to selected clients,' came the voice through the partially opened door. It was Alex at his sexiest, voice oozing through the crack in the door like rich cream.

'Who is this guy?' Anna's eyes sparkled with interest as Helen clung stubbornly to her position, feeling somewhat foolish, but determined to keep the wolf from her door.

'Alex Knight.'

'Greg's brother? Alex Knight the writer? The one we saw interviewed last night on TV?' Anna's voice sank to a conspiratorial whisper. 'The Incredible Hunk? And you're trying to send him *away*? What are you, crazy?'

'This is supposed to be a shower——'

'Honey, I'll shower with Alex Knight any day! Besides, we're all out of wine anyway.' With a cunning feint Anna elbowed Helen out of the way and threw the door wide.

'Hi, Alex, I'm Anna . . . I'm a nurse, I'm twenty-four and I'm single and heart-whole.'

'Hold out your other hand, Anna, the one with the engagement ring on it,' said Helen sourly as Alex gallantly kissed the proffered hand.

'Isn't it the way?' said Alex wistfully. 'The one woman in the world I fall in love with, and she's already promised to another.' He spoke to Anna but his eyes were on Helen's face and she felt herself blushing angrily. Fortunately, Anna noticed nothing amiss.

'Is that the champers? Is it cold? Mmmm, lovely. God, I wish you were going to be *my* brother-in-law. Steve has four brothers and all they ever bring is beer for themselves. Count your blessings, Helen, dear! Come on in, Alex, and meet the girls.'

Helen found herself trailing behind the other two. 'You shouldn't be here,' she muttered to Alex's shoulder-blades. 'I thought you'd decided to stay away.'

'Miss me?' he taunted softly, over his shoulder.

'No!' How could she, when he had been with her in spirit all the time, whispering like a serpent into her ear, magnifying the normal bridal jitters into jolts that measured on the Richter scale?

Predictably, 'the girls' were delighted by the arrival of a personable male in their midst, especially one who took no offence at their well-wined outrageousness. Helen, who had imbibed the least of any of them, reluctantly accepted a glass of champagne and watched with irritation as Alex expertly juggled six simultaneous flirtations. His technique promised everything and delivered nothing. And that about summed up Alexander Knight, she decided fiercely.

'Aren't you going to open his present, Helen?' said Nicola when she managed to tear her attention away from Alex's masculine charms.

She didn't want to. She sensed danger emanating from the large silver-wrapped parcel. She couldn't imagine Alex settling for an ordinary gift. He would want it to be as unique as he was...

'Go on, Helen,' urged Serena, whose generous employer had flown her back from Wellington, where the family were temporarily settled, to be at her flatmate's shower. Serena, who had retained a childlike delight in surprises that was probably one of the many reasons that she got on so well with her charges, began to pick at the knotted ribbon with a clear-glossed nail, until Anna batted her away.

'It's Helen's present, she gets to open it.'

'Well, hurry up, Helen.' Serena consoled herself with another glass of champagne and a pretty smile at a receptive Alex. 'I'm dying to know what the lovely man has given you.'

Lovely man, indeed! Would he be such a hit with her friends if they knew he had been trying to wreck her engagement?

She had been right to be wary. The brown cardboard box, filled with shredded paper, held an exquisite piece of porcelain, A Lladro angel.

'Not exactly suitable for a kitchen shower,' said Helen shakily into the expectant silence as she turned the beautiful piece gently in her hands. The slender, golden-haired angel was tall, her face divinely serene, the detail in her wings and robe extremely fine. Helen knew it must have cost a fortune.

'But singularly appropriate,' said Alex, and Helen stiffened, in case any one else picked up that peculiarly gentle note in his voice. But her friends were too busy admiring the gift.

'It's gorgeous, Helen,' said Nicola enviously. 'And you're right, Alex, it's very appropriate. Go and get *his* gift, Helen.'

'Oh, no, I——'

'A gift? For me? What is it?' Alex looked both surprised and touchingly eager.

'Go on, Helen, let him see it,' Nicola urged. 'You'll love it, Alex...'

Forced into a corner, Helen went off to fetch the sweater, regretting that she had ever started it. She didn't really know why she had knitted it, when there were rush-orders going begging, but she had told herself that she wasn't giving Alex any of her customers' time since she had worked on it at night, putting off going to sleep until she was bleary-eyed and dropping stitches with the effort. It was Alex who had caused her disruptive dreams, it had seemed fitting that she used him to fill in the time that would be otherwise spent brooding.

'I've still got a couple of seams to finish off,' she said as she came back into the lounge, putting off the moment when she would have to satisfy the curiosity in Alex's eyes. Not that he didn't look satisfied already... smug, even. She wished that she had never cast the wretched thing on. Now he would *know* she had been thinking about him. He would think that she had done it for *him* rather than Hannah, who hadn't been willing to let the subject drop.

She held up the sweater. It was a mohair and wool mix, very light and soft in a plain black stocking-stitch. Below the V-neck, half-way down the chest, was an ap-pliquéd halo, done in a velvety gold fabric wound with glittering gold and silver cord.

Alex got up from where he had been sprawling on the floor cushions, his dark eyes lighting with admiration and pleasure. 'It's marvellous, Helen. You're very talented. It's just what I imagined, except better...'

Helen couldn't help feeling exhilarated at his unin-hibited flattery.

'It's reversible, too,' said Nicola with a grin. 'Show him the other side, Helen.'

Helen hesitated, and Alex, intrigued by her expression of green-eyed mischief and misgiving, took a step closer. Hurriedly Helen reversed the sweater and shook it out. Appliquéd to the chest now, in red quilted satin, were horns and a pitchfork and arrow tail.

Alex began to laugh. 'I love it! So I can wear it according to my mood. Or is it supposed to be symbolic of the devil within us all? Did you think I need reminding that none of us is all good, or all bad? Will it take long to finish? I'd love to wear it.'

'It's the middle of summer,' Helen protested.

'I can do it for you right now, if you like,' said Nicola, whisking the sweater away from Helen. 'You can wear it home.'

'It's blazing hot out there,' said Helen. She had never before felt possessive of her work; it was, after all, made to be worn. But somehow the thought of Alex actually putting on the sweater she had made him was symbolic of more than just another job finished. He would be a Knight, wearing his lady's colours.

'I'll wait until it's cold and dark before I leave,' he said. 'And I'll take my T-shirt off and wear it next to my skin.'

Helen pictured the soft friction of wool against firm, smooth gold skin, and shivered at the sensual portrait of her handiwork caressing the rippling muscles of his chest. He would have to wait months before the weather got colder. Six months cooped up in a small apartment with Alex, eating, sleeping, living in intimate human contact. Helen's stomach tightened. A few months from now she would be an old married woman, possibly even pregnant. Alex would be uncle to her child, there would be a blood tie between them. The idea made Helen feel queasy. She had somehow thought that once she married Greg, Alex would go back off to his own life and be out of her life for good. But what if, having re-established his family links, he became a regular visitor? A spectre at the wedding feast was bad enough, but the prospect of a permanent haunting was unbearable. Whenever she saw him she would be reminded of her guilty knowledge and their conspiracy of silence about it. It would be like indulging in a form of retroactive adultery!

'Helen?' Helen blinked. 'Daydreaming?' Alex's hard mouth curved, and she realised that she had been staring again. 'Was it something I said?'

His smug look told her that he knew it was. He enjoyed his ability to violate her peace of mind. Helen pulled herself together and began tidying away the presents that she had received. Her guests began to make reluctant noises about leaving, as Alex showed no signs of broaching the second bottle of champagne. Helen noted that their farewells to Alex were a great deal fonder than their cheerful leave-taking of herself, and he showed no objection to being warmly kissed on the mouth by three of them. She wondered tartly whether Alex's interpretation of chastity was a lot looser than other people's, and then was disgusted with herself for being cynical about a few innocent kisses. But she couldn't help remembering that when Alex had kissed *her* she had felt anything but innocent! She certainly hadn't felt like laughing, the way her friends did as they floated out the door.

In the midst of cleaning up the litter of plates and cups and glasses, Serena peered at her watch and announced that her flight to Wellington was leaving in thirty-eight minutes. There was a scramble to phone for a taxi, and Anna, noting the way her friend was swaying on her feet, offered to accompany her to make sure she got on to the right plane.

'Leave all this stuff until I get back,' said Anna, waving at the debris as she hustled a giggling Serena towards the door. 'And don't worry if I'm a little bit late...if Gerry's due off duty he can give me a lift back.' Anna's fiancé was a Customs officer at the airport.

In the panic to repack the contents of the overnight bag that Serena had managed to scatter far and wide through the apartment since her arrival the previous day, Helen had no time to consider the implications of Anna's offer, but after the door had closed on Serena's slightly slurred promise to make it back for the wedding, she suddenly realised that the situation she had hoped to avoid for the next week had occurred. She and Alex were alone.

Reluctantly she turned back into the apartment. In the lounge she found with a small shock that Alex was trying on the sweater, his hard stomach concave below the arch of his ribcage as he lifted his arms to shrug into the sleeves. From his navel a line of soft, crisp curls a shade darker than the hair on his head divided the tanned skin of his lower belly, thickening as they dived under the low-slung band of his jeans. He made a throaty sound of pleasure as the sweater slid down over his chest and hips, discreetly veiling the blatant masculinity outlined by his tight jeans.

'Mmm, it feels as good as it looks.'

Helen noted with misgiving that he was wearing it devil-side out. 'I'm glad you like it,' she said stiffly.

'How much do I owe you?'

She scowled at him. 'Nothing, it's a gift.' Nicola had told her that she couldn't possibly charge him for it.

'Thank you, Helen. What a lovely thought.'

'It wasn't my idea,' she told him stubbornly, but he only chuckled.

'But you carried it through. It was very gracious of you, in the circumstances.'

She cleared her throat, conscious of the silence in the apartment after the noise of the afternoon. *The circumstances.* In the circumstances, the wisest thing to do would be to hustle him out the door as quickly as possible. To hell with being gracious, she didn't want Alexander Knight here in her apartment, making her think dangerous thoughts. He took no notice of her hesitation. He began to pick up the dirty crockery and carry it through to the kitchen.

'What are you doing?'

'Helping you clear up. You have a well-developed sense of responsibility. I don't imagine that you're going to leave all this for Anna, not after she went to all the trouble of organising this little gathering for you.'

'You don't have to do that. I can manage. I don't suppose you're very domesticated,' she said firmly, going over and taking the cups out of his hand. He merely turned and scooped up some others, following her through to the small, grey and white tiled kitchen with its bright red bench.

'Oh, you'd be surprised how domesticated I can be, given the incentive,' he murmured, rattling around in the cupboards to find the washing-up liquid and sponge-mop.

Helen gave up protesting and went to gather the rest of the plates. She was *not* going to ask what kind of incentives he required. She sensed she wouldn't like the answer.

He was humming as he washed up, the sleeves of the sweater safely pushed up out of harm's way. He didn't look so out of place doing dishes, she realised, but then, she had difficulty imagining that Alex would look out of place *anywhere*; he was nothing if not adaptable.

'You've used too much washing-up liquid,' she said as she took a towel. It gave her confidence to find fault.

He stacked another soapy glass on to the draining tray. 'At least you know these things will be clean. This stuff is like love, better too much than too little.'

She couldn't think of a reply to that, so she stayed silent, drying the cup in her hand with such force that the handle came off.

'Hmmm, I think you're the undomesticated one,' said Alex as she thrust the damaged cup to the back of the cupboard. 'I hope you're more careful when you dust my angel.'

'You shouldn't have spent so much.'

'I hadn't planned to,' he deflated her protest. 'But I saw her in a shop window and I remembered that Mum said you collected Lladro figures. She reminded me so much of you that I couldn't leave her to be bought by somebody to whom she would be just another piece.'

'She doesn't look at all like me,' Helen said. 'She's tall and slender and blonde...in fact, she's nothing like me at all.'

'Inside she is,' he said softly. 'Inside she's tender and sweet and strong and compassionate and, most of all, loving of the undeserving.' At her choked sound of protest he held up a soapy hand. 'She is also a beautiful piece of work and should go to someone who can truly appreciate the craftsmanship involved. How did you first get interested in collecting?'

His question effectively defused the tension, and Helen found herself telling him about her visit to Spain. She and her friends had been mini-vanning around southern Europe at the time, camping rough to eke out their funds, and there had been no room for souvenirs in their cramped van, let alone delicate porcelainware, so Helen had had to curb her desire for ownership until she got back to New Zealand.

'I haven't got all that much yet, because I've done so much moving around it was rather pointless to buy something just to pack it away in storage whenever I took off.'

'I own my possessions, they do not own me,' murmured Alex. 'I felt the same way, when I was a correspondent. I owned nothing I couldn't carry...which was one reason I got so rich so quickly...there's only so much you can spend on food and drink and hotels. I invested the rest in property...after getting an inside track on some of the skilled stock manipulations of less-than-savoury financiers and their bankers and brokers, I determined never to rely on a "paper fortune". I own the place where I live in New York, and in the past few years I've been slowly building up a solid home for myself rather than just using it as a base of operations. I doubt whether I'd get my possessions in forty suitcases now. I guess you might say that I have given myself a stake in the world's future. I find myself these days obeying without thought the rules of society that, ten years ago, I thought were laid down for the sole purpose of denying my individuality.' He grinned. 'My friends call it "calming down".'

'If you're calm now, I would hate to have known you ten years ago,' said Helen.

'I would, too. I had precious few illusions and a crusading desire to shatter those of others. I hadn't realised that illusions are very necessary to the survival of the human spirit; from our illusions come our greatest hopes, our drive to better ourselves, to reach for the stars.' Wickedness glinted in the brown eyes as he threw down the dish-mop, let the water drain away and turned to catch her watching him, grave and wistful.

'Besides, ten years ago you were only fourteen, much too young for me. You were probably still skinny and tomboyish, with no breasts to speak of...'

Helen blushed furiously as he laughed. He had described her exactly at fourteen.

'It's a shame your parents aren't alive to see what a beautiful woman their little girl grew up to be.' He switched moods again, and to her horror Helen found a slight sting behind her eyes at his gentle sincerity. Damn him, he made her angry with him and then he took her totally off guard with his unexpected understanding. Her parents would have been so happy for her to be marrying such a 'nice' man as Greg. They would have made marvellous grandparents. Even after all this time Helen still missed their warmth and undemanding love. She could do with some of her mother's down-to-earth advice right now!

Helen put down her tea towel. Damn it! She was letting Alex direct her thoughts and actions yet again.

'What are you doing here, Alex? Why did you come? You could have given your mother your present to bring and, considering the way you've been carrying on, the champagne was rather a hypocritical touch——'

'I toasted your happiness. Nothing hypocritical about that. I want you to be happy, I just don't believe that you will be if you marry Greg. And he's the reason I'm here.'

Apprehension struck. 'Greg is? What's the matter? What's wrong?'

'Relax, unfortunately he hasn't changed his mind about marrying you next week. But he *is* back from Bangkok.'

'I know. He called me this morning. So what?'

'So, our agreement is voided.'

'Agreement, what agreement?'

'That I would stay away from you, as long as he was away.'

'What?' In the small kitchen the word was explosively loud.

'He didn't trust me in your company while he was in Bangkok, or perhaps it was *you* he didn't trust,' Alex taunted her. 'So we made a bargain.'

'You made a *bargain*, over *me*? The two of you? Without *telling* me?' Helen's outrage was impossible to contain, it brimmed over in stormy grey clouds in her green eyes, a rash of temper covering her face and throat and shoulders. She had to move. She had to pace off her fury. If the memory of her self-righteous lecture at the party wasn't vivid in her brain, she would have lashed out at Alex's infuriatingly handsome face. Instead she shoved him aside and fled the claustrophobic kitchen. In the lounge she looked around for something convenient to throw to exercise her rage. Her eye fell on the

Lladro angel, a porcelain lady who never lost her cool, representative of all her problems.

'You wouldn't, would you?' asked Alex quietly. 'Destroy something so lovely just to hurt me?'

Helen swung around. Now he was reading her thoughts from the back of her head! Was there nothing she could hide from him? 'Why should it hurt *you*? It's mine—I can do what I want with it.'

He shrugged. 'It's your decision, of course.' And, having bowed to her right to behave as she pleased, he burdened her with the responsibility for her own action. Of course she couldn't destroy it ... not because *he* had given it to her, but because it was a thing of great beauty, she told herself.

'How dare you ... haggle over my company as if I had no say in the matter?' she returned to the root of her anger. 'It's degrading. It's worse than being fought over! It reduces me to a ... a ... *possession*. And it's all your fault ... stirring Greg up with your damned interference. You could have come around here ten times a day and it wouldn't have made a blind bit of difference to me! Nothing will change the way I feel about Greg.'

'Greg obviously isn't as confident as you,' said Alex reasonably. 'Perhaps he's projecting his own doubts on to you to give them an outlet he finds acceptable.'

Helen wasn't going to touch that one with a bargepole.

'If Greg has any doubts, he can discuss them with me himself. We don't need a third party to adjudicate, thank you very much,' she said sarcastically. 'Especially a hatchet-man with an axe to grind.'

'Don't get sore at me, Helen. The whole agreement was Greg's idea. All I said was that I was in love with you and intended to do my damnedest to steal you from him ... but honourably, no sneaking around behind his back and lying about my intentions. I wasn't going to do it by "befriending" you the way he had my lonely wife. For one thing, I have a rather urgent deadline...'

'Oh, my God,' Helen covered her appalled eyes with her hands, shutting out his rueful smile. 'How *could* you? No wonder Greg was so quiet when I told him——'

'Told him what?' Alex was quick to pick up the remark she bit off a few words too late. 'What have you told him, Helen?'

She lowered her hands. 'What I said I would.' Her eyes sparkled with defiance. 'That I'm not a virgin, after all.'

His eyes narrowed. 'Is that all? And what delicate shade of whitewash did you use to explain away the stain on your...er...imagined purity of body and soul?'

'I didn't lie,' she told him fiercely. 'I said I'd been to the doctor, which is true, for...for contraceptive advice and that she told me that I wasn't...wasn't...'

'Intact?' suggested Alex with mock delicacy.

'I told him that I had no recollection of how or when it happened, but that it must have been before my operation and he accepted it.'

'Just like that?'

'Just like that. I told you he wouldn't treat it like a federal case for investigation.' In fact, Greg had taken the news rather *too* quietly on the drive to the airport, just patting her hand and quickly assuring her that of course it made no difference to them, although of course it was a bit of a shock. Helen had felt a trifle cheated, after all her soul-searching and rehearsing of the difficult little speech. She had got the feeling that she could have told him that she had been a former streetwalker and he would have said the same thing, so anxious had he been to keep things smooth and on an even course while he was away. Now she knew why. He had been worrying about what Alex might get up to, determined that he find no loophole in their relationship to exploit.

'He must have been rather chagrined that you've been holding back from him what you gave to somebody else...'

'For your information, it hasn't been *me* who's been holding back!' Helen blurted out triumphantly.

'Is that so?' Alex's eyes took on a peculiar glow. 'How very noble and misguided of him. I suppose now he'll be anxious to redress the situation.'

Helen tilted her head proudly, her glossy hair brushing across the top of her slender shoulders. 'As a matter of fact, no. He said that we may as well wait for the wedding now.'

'Really?' Now Alex was definitely intrigued by his brother's state of mind. 'I wonder whether that's for his sake or yours.'

'What does that mean?'

'Do you really want to know?' Alex's mouth was curved wryly, and suddenly Helen *didn't* want to know. 'Suffice it to say that if that was my ring on your finger, you wouldn't be able to keep me out of your bed. Odd, if the sexual chemistry between you is so intense, that you both find it so easy to resist.'

'I never said that!'

'What, that it's intense? Or that it's easy to resist?' he taunted. 'Whirlwind courtships like yours are usually filled with whirlwind passion. Perhaps you've both held back because, subconsciously, you fear disappointment when you finally *do* get into bed. Maybe you need the spur of commitment first, because you sense that the sparks between you are artificially generated and wouldn't outlast a trial relationship. You decided soon after you met Greg that your affinity for each other was love, and that has blinkered the natural development of your relationship. You're locked in by the precepts of your upbringing, and by your misconceptions about yourselves and each other to a course of action that could ruin a fine friendship. Do you think I can't see that your reactions to Greg are only a shadow of your reaction to me? With him you feel warm and happy and secure, all fine in their way but not for you...with me you can have fire, joy and the thrill of knowing you affect me in the same way that I affect you.'

He was twisting her feelings for Greg into unrecognisable knots, the slow, certain voice hammering away at her vulnerable defences.

'You're wrong, dead wrong,' she said jerkily, seeing him as a silhouette in front of an aching void. One step and she would be lost in the terrifying land of the unknown, one concession and the little army of fears and doubts would come marching out of the dark, forgotten corners of her mind. 'I love Greg and I'll be a good wife to him.'

'Damned by faint ambition.' Floundering in the deep darkness of his gaze, Helen didn't notice him stalking closer. 'Don't you want to be more than just a "good wife", Helen? Home, children, financial security...I can understand you wanting all those things, but you could have them with me. Is it fair to give Greg the credit for evoking needs and desires that *I* created, five years ago?' His hands were on her wrists, sliding up her silky arms to her shoulders, tilting her mesmerised body towards his in the process.

'No,' she whispered automatically, but he continued in the deep, hypnotic voice.

'You might not remember me, Helen, but I'm there, inside you, ticking away like a time-bomb. What happens on this long-awaited wedding night of yours if Greg's lovemaking triggers the mechanism of your memory? What if when he touches you it's *my* hands you feel stroking you, what if when he sighs it's *my* love-groans that fill your ears? Can you make love to two men at the same time, Helen? How will you know which one you're responding to?'

The silken words wrapped round and round her, binding her to the melting heat of his body... closer... closer, until she felt as if she was being absorbed by him, into his singing bloodstream, flesh of his flesh. His hands moved lightly over her back, cupping her shoulder-blades to move her round breasts against his chest, crushing and massaging her body with his. He swayed with her in an erotic dance, his thighs surrounding hers as one hand cupped the nape of her neck and tilted her dreamy face up to his.

'Who am I?' he asked against her mouth.

'Alex?' The terrible implications of his words suddenly sank into her hazy brain, the ugly reality of what he was saying. 'No——'

'Yes.' His tongue stroked away her muffled protest, his teeth burrowing lightly into the fullness of her lower lips, taking small, delicious bites out of her resistance. 'Alex... you know me, don't you? In your heart you know... I was the one who drew first blood, Angel. I was the one you turned to in your need, who showed you the glory of being a woman. And how you loved me for it... all through the long night. How hot and sweet you were, and eager, so eager to know everything. You were the most uninhibited lover I've ever had... my best lover... my last lover... my once and only lover...'

His long, slow, hot kisses filled her senses with the touch, the scent and taste of him until they brimmed over and little fires licked along her skin, her breasts flowering to aching fullness against his chest, the soft mounds swelling tautly above the boned cotton of her bodice. He touched them, lightly, and she made a sighing sound in his mouth that he answered with a groan. She felt the zip at her back parting, the confining bodice slipping away, and she twisted in protest. He broke the kiss, eyes glittering with fierce pleasure, his skin flushed and damp, mouth sensually bruised as he twisted too, shuddering as the hard peaks of her breasts scraped against him. Impatiently he pulled off his sweater and repeated the gesture. The soft scattering of body hair created an erotic friction far more exciting than that of the mohair and wool, and Helen felt her skin stretch so unbearably tight, she felt as if she was going to explode.

'Alex——' She clutched at him convulsively, not knowing whether she was rejecting or inviting his touch. But he knew...

'It's all right, darling,' he whispered against the delicate curve of her jaw. 'I know what you want, I know where you like to be touched, and how... I know everything about how to please you...' And his fingers wound into her hair, pulling her head back so that her spine arched against the hand that held her hips against his arousal. His tongue tracked the blue vein that traced a creamy breast until he found the rosy crest, where he nipped and licked until her hands pleadingly cupped his head and he began to suckle with rhythmic firmness that made her almost faint with pleasure. Her legs sagged until she was cradled against the hardness between his thighs as he turned his attention to her other breast and loved it with equal fervour and skill.

'Alex!' Her cry of bewilderment and fear checked his quest for mutual satisfaction, her hand clenching painfully in his hair as her body stormed out of control.

'It's all right, Angel. Shhh, it's going to be all right.' He soothed her with kisses as he buried her moist and fiery nipples in his chest, thrusting a muscled thigh between her legs to help ease the ache that convulsed her body. His own body craved the contact, pulsed with hot, heavy male need. He had her helpless in his arms, crying out for what only he would give her, and the urge to set the seal on their passion was almost overwhelming. But once having had her again he would not be capable of leaving. He had waited five years for this, he was not going to ruin the only chance he might have to gain her trust for the sake of fleeting relief from the hunger that prowled in his loins.

'There . . . better?' His voice and hands were gentle as they petted and caressed, and slowly brought her back to a semblance of sanity, hiding his exultation behind an expression of sensuous tenderness. 'God, you're beautiful.' He looked with pleasure at her semi-nudity, unable to stop himself cupping one quivering breast and saluting its loveliness with a farewell kiss as he slowly drew up her dress and re-zipped it. Dressing her was quite as erotic and threatening to his self-control as undressing her.

'You called out my name,' he said, supporting her with firm hands on her waist as she blinked misty green eyes at him. 'Just now, when your eyes were closed and you were drowning in bliss. You like to talk in bed, my darling Angel, and with me you don't have to pretend, you don't have to curb your thoughts or tongue, or fear you might call out another name in the heat of the moment if you let yourself go. *Mine* is the name you associate with sexual fulfilment, not Greg's. When you're with him, will you call him by my name?'

He held her eyes, watching the dawning of knowledge, the realisation of what had just happened and with whom, and who had been the first to draw back. And then his words began to bite, and her eyes slanted with pain, the huge, dark pupils contracting with shock.

'A time-bomb, Helen, and the timer is already set. Perhaps even now, some memories are surfacing?' His hands tightened on her waist as she flinched, tearing her eyes away from his.

'No——'

'Not even a little flash?'

'*No.*' She was struggling in earnest now, panicking at what he was trying to force her to admit.

'And yet you flowered in my arms like a desert bloom in the rain. I could have taken you, *still* could——' he moved his hips against hers, showing that his desire had not lessened '—and we both know you'd welcome me. But I want more than welcome. I don't want to be a guest in your life, Helen, I wanted to be invited in . . . I want you to do the inviting.' He took her hand and pressed it against himself, and she trembled at the raw, restrained power that was encompassed in her hand.

She tried to pull her hand away and he groaned, his body clenching as he let her go. She backed away, shaking, savaged by a torrent of emotion.

'No! Never . . . I would never hurt Greg. I——' The words stuck in her dry throat. 'He loves me.'

'Does he? Or is he, like you, just reaching out for someone to hold on to, someone to appease his loneliness, to flesh out the hollows of his life? He doesn't love you, Helen, because he's still hung up on Alice. It's Alice he wants, he's always wanted, but because he thinks he can't have her he'll settle for second best . . . just as you are.'

'You're lying.' Helen shook her head jerkily. 'You're just saying that——'

'There'll be four in that wedding bed, Helen . . . you and me and Greg and Alice. You're a substitute, that's why he's afraid to make love to you before the wedding. He wants to put off facing the reality, the *finality*, of what he's doing until he has no choice. He hasn't changed.'

'That's not true,' Helen panted, clasping her arms about herself to stop the awful shivering that chilled her body.

'Has he ever made love to you the way I just did? Enjoyed your body the way I have? Oh, superficially all the chemistry is there, but I suspect it's been mostly on your side. Has he ever looked at you the way I have? Excited you the way I have? Stroked your lovely naked breasts and watched the way they swell and harden, pleading to be kissed and suckled——'

'Stop it! Stop it!' Helen spun around, her hands over her ears, body hunched over to protect herself from the shame of revealing that even his words had the ability to arouse her. No, Greg had never taken their love-making so far... but that was because he respected her. He had touched her through her clothes, and a few times had slid his hands under her top, but usually that was under cover of darkness during their passionate good-nights in the car, or by romantic candlelight in his apartment. She had never once thought there was anything odd about Greg not wanting to strip her in broad daylight and watch the effects of his light loving on her body. He had been considerate of her blushes, rather than inhibited. Alex was just trying to confuse her with those ugly claims about Alice. All her doubts about his motives for behaving as if he was madly in love with her came rushing back in full force, battering her badly bruised emotions.

'I want you to go, I want you to get out, now... or I'll call Greg and tell him what you've been saying. Or is that what you want?' She looked at him with something close to hatred for what he was doing, and he knew it was time to withdraw.

'All I want is for you and Greg to be honest with each other.'

'*All* you want?' she asked bitterly.

'It's a start. You and I belong, Helen. One day you'll recognise that, and I just hope it won't be too late for both of us. I'm going.' He bent and picked up the sweater from the floor, and his T-shirt from the couch. The flex of his muscles was reminiscent of the sleekness of a powerful, predatory animal stretching triumphantly after the excitement of the kill, his golden pelt glossy with health. He put on the T-shirt, which only emphasised the male sculpture beneath. 'But I won't go away, Helen. What's between us won't go away either, however much you try to sweep it under the carpet.'

'Alex——' She wasn't sure why she stopped him as he reached for the door, and when he turned she was suddenly flustered by the expression of hope which sat oddly on his cynical years. It made him look years younger... five years younger... a face in sleep that was cleansed of care, incongruously innocent, trusting... an impression that was abruptly dispelled when the brown eyes fluttered open, the heavy lids lifting, a sensuous appraisal translated into erotic actions, warm and languorous in the tangled bed.

Oh, God, no! Helen stared at him in horror. *No, please don't let him be right, please don't let this happen now!*

'Your champagne,' she stammered. 'You forgot the other bottle of champagne.'

He looked at her pale face curiously. 'You keep it,' he said. 'Save it for the wedding. Our wedding.'

And he left her alone with her memories.

CHAPTER EIGHT

HE HADN'T looked at all innocent or trusting when she had first seen him. He had looked lean and mean, as if he didn't believe in anything or anyone, including himself. There had been a hard, cruel edge to his handsome features as he had stood, a brooding island in the midst of a sea of jollity, surveying the rest of the partygoers with sullen contempt. His bitter black eyes were never still, roving, searching...for what? A woman? He looked like a man who knew a lot about women...maybe too much. Helen had hurriedly crossed him off her list of potentials. She didn't want a man so harsh and jaded that he just went through the motions, no matter how good-looking he was. She wanted someone who was sensitive, kind, someone on whom she could try out her fledgling sexuality without being made to feel either inadequate or cheap.

She knew it was a tall order for a one-night stand, but she had high hopes of success. The figure-hugging ice-blue dress that she had bought late that afternoon for a hideous number of Hong Kong dollars—thanks to Susan's wide-ranging credit—had already attracted a few pleasant possibilities, and the mild-mannered young man that Susan had dug up to escort her to the sophisticated gathering at the American Club at Tai Tam Bay had obligingly vanished when she had told him that she wouldn't be requiring a lift back to the Hilton.

Helen's problem was that she didn't just want *pleasant*, she wanted *special*. She wanted a man who could sweep her off her feet, and vice versa. This experience might have to last a long time...possibly for eternity. Helen

141

felt reckless...deliciously wicked. She had been a sweet, virtuous girl for every one of her nineteen years, and now she wanted to know what she had been missing. The crazy idea that had only occurred to her that morning, when she had shared the lift at the Hilton with a pair of blissfully amorous newly-weds, had hardened into implacable determination. If it took her all night, she was going to find herself a man!

Then the tall, bitter-eyed stranger had looked across the room at her and smiled. The curve of his mouth was a sensual promise that sent a tingle through her too-slender body, and she stared at him in wonder and regret. What a pity he wasn't suitable.

The tingling became a steady, pulsing electric current when the man began pushing his way towards her, ignoring several attractive women who cast themselves across his path. *He was coming over.* Helen felt her palms go damp as she wondered how she was going to brush him off. He didn't look like a man who took too kindly to rejection. He looked like trouble with a capital T.

She didn't look at him until he came to a stop in front of her, pretending a nonchalance she didn't feel. And then, when she did, she was lost. *His eyes.* The recognition was instant and overwhelming. In his eyes there was more than mere bitterness, there was emptiness, bewilderment, desperation. There was an insolent sexuality, too, as he looked over her body in the wispy, glittery dress, but her awareness was more than merely sexual. The recognition was total—the empathy such that she felt his pain, the pain of a man on the brink of breaking.

He was swaying slightly on his feet, compensating for it by the aggressive set of his shoulders and slashing jaw. She had noticed that he had been drinking steadily, but no one would dare call him drunk. A tough customer, which made the devastation behind the angry eyes so much more shattering. Helen wanted to reach out and

touch him and reassure him that he wasn't alone... that
loneliness shared was loneliness halved. Then he spoke,
his voice as sultry as his eyes, a whisky-flavoured rasp.

'Want to come to bed with me, green eyes?'

Helen heard a slight gasp from the couple beside her,
but she ignored their disapproval. A hot flush joined the
electric tingling in her body. He wanted her, that much
was obvious from the way he was staring at her high,
rounded breasts as if he could already taste them, but
she sensed that his crudeness was designed to offend.
Why, then, had he come over? Strangely, she didn't feel
at all threatened by his aggression. She felt... excited...

Recklessness gripped her anew. Why not? Tonight was
a night for breaking the rules. She consigned her mental
list to oblivion and smiled at him, her green eyes warming
to the colour of a sun-washed sea.

'I'll just get my wrap and bag,' she told him, with
grave amusement at the shock, swiftly followed by a
hard, hungry desire, that swept across his face. She
turned from the open-mouthed couple and began to
make her way back to where she had checked in her
things, conscious of the tall figure shadowing her every
step. She was committed now; she wouldn't allow herself
any second thoughts. The stranger with the haunted eyes
had been handed to her by fate, and she would make
the most of the gift. Instinctively she knew that, despite
the aura of suppressed violence about him, he wouldn't
hurt her.

He was suffering in some way, and seeking ease in the
fleeting pleasures of the flesh while cynically doubting
that he would find it. If he hurt anyone, it would be
himself. Helen sensed depths of feeling in him that were
at odds with his handsome dissipation. Even just 'going
through the motions' with a woman, he would be an
exciting lover, taking masculine satisfaction in fulfilling
his partner, if not himself. Helen didn't intend to let that
happen. She was flooded with a tender thrill of antici-

pation. Perhaps tonight wouldn't be merely a practical physical experiment, after all...perhaps she could make it something more. Perhaps she could give, as well as take, from the situation, and thus release herself from the last bonds of conscience.

The long taxi-ride around the bays and through the glittering night-lights of the compact, towering city to the cross harbour tunnel gave her plenty of time to get nervous, for the man never said a word after he had directed the driver to take them to the Regent Hotel, in Kowloon. He sat in his corner of the back seat and stared at her. She, not having any store of sophisticated patter, merely stared back, again feeling the urge to reassure him, when really it should be Helen who needed the reassuring.

When they got to his hotel room he was no more talkative. He went straight into the drinks, pouring himself a Scotch and drinking it in a single gulp before he offered her one. She refused, and he gave an insolent shrug, pouring himself another.

'Dutch courage?' she enquired coolly, her heart thumping in her chest, wondering if she hadn't made a mistake, after all, with all her fantasising about this moment. Maybe he was an alcoholic. Maybe one drink was the difference between a man lost to himself and a ravening beast!

The drink froze inches from his mouth. 'What in the hell would a woman like you know about courage, Dutch or otherwise?' he ground out savagely.

'I know it can't sustain itself in isolation,' she said quietly, remembering vividly the time when she had lashed out angrily at sympathy and support, the resentment of the walking wounded for those who were whole and well. A wry smile drifted across her soft mouth, wide in her thin face. 'I know the times that you most need it are the times you doubt it the most.'

There was a brief, stark silence, and then the whisky travelled to his lips and he took a long pull. In spite of the weary lines on his face, he looked like a sulky teenager defying sound parental advice.

'Well, what are you waiting for?' he demanded as she merely stood, watching him with wise eyes, eyes that seemed to see everything, every weakness and every flaw. He flung himself on to the cream velvet couch and sat there, white dinner-jacket splayed against the upholstery, feet planted squarely on the pale blue carpet, wide apart so that she was aware of his insolent maleness. 'Take off the dress…slowly. Show me what you've got.'

He was lashing himself, not her. It was himself he wanted to despise, to degrade. Helen felt a welling compassion that obliterated any feelings of virginal embarrassment. She put her hands behind her and slid down the zip. The dress slithered off her shoulders and merged into the carpet at her feet, leaving her in a delicate strapless bra of lavender stretch lace, and matching briefs with a triangular silk V supported by narrow bands of lace cut high across her narrow thighs. The weight she had lost in recent months emphasised rather than diminished the feminine curves that were left, making her slender legs look longer and her breasts fuller. Her skin was hospital pale beneath the olive toning, and the silver-blonde of her hair complimented her doll-like femininity.

'And the rest,' he said, in a brittle voice which pierced her to the heart. She stepped across the glittering evidence of her fallen modesty and knelt between his outstretched legs. She took his drink from him and placed it on the table beside the couch. She took the hand she had freed and held it to her lace-covered breast, letting him feel the warmth, the steady beat of her heart as it measured the rhythm of her life. Her eyes were shy in their boldness, green and grave and seductive in more ways than one.

'Help me,' she asked softly. 'I'm lost, you see... I've never done this before...'

He shouldn't have believed her, but he did. Against all the odds, he believed her simple statement. He looked helplessly into her innocent gaze and groaned, beginning to shake, beginning to break up inside. His head fell back, the cords in his neck standing out in tortured relief against his tanned throat, his face contorting as the words were torn from him. 'Help you? God, how can I help you when I can't even help myself? You'd better go... don't let me touch you...' His hand contracted involuntarily on her breast, but it wasn't a sexual gesture, it was a painful spasm that gripped his entire body. 'I'll only hurt you... I don't know how to be gentle any more... I've lost it... I can't... I can't *see* anything any more but pain and blood. I... don't let me drag you down there with me. God, I'm so sick of my life... Where did all the dreams go?'

How could she have forgotten the feel of a man's tears against her skin, the taste of them in her mouth as she had kissed and rocked away his anguish? She had never seen a man, before or since, in such mental pain that it manifested itself in physical helplessness, never seen a human being so vulnerable, so stripped bare of all defences. Perhaps the amount of whisky he had consumed contributed in part to the destruction of what had obviously been an iron self-control, but Helen had the feeling that it was more than that. Something about her had touched something in him, drawn him into the vortex of his own, long repressed feelings. She felt responsible, so she held him tightly as he shuddered and sweated like a man in the choking grip of a delirium, his body racked with spasms as he vomited forth a corrosive stream of words that sketched a picture of a man driven beyond endurance by the sick hatreds and blood-soaked horrors that he had forced himself to witness in the name of truth. Only now there was no truth, no right or wrong, no place in him untouched by the cruelty, the filth and corruption of the series of hells, small and large, where he had spent the last few years of his life. There was no longer any refuge or escape inside himself, no resources left to draw on. He could no longer repress the guilt at being a bystander to atrocities he relived in sickening detail, the pain and fear that had become constant companions finally paralysing his will and even his imagination. He no longer felt like a functioning human being, but a machine, endlessly recording variations on the same horrific theme over and over again...

When he finally fell asleep, stretched out on the couch, still held tightly against Helen's compassionate breast, she had cried hot, silent tears of pity and relief that he had finally found the peace to rest...a luxury he had not allowed himself in a very long time. Towards the end of his talking jag his voice had grown hoarse and finally thready as exhaustion conquered his compulsive confession, and heavy lids fluttered down over glazed brown eyes as he turned his damp face into the soft comfort of her woman's flesh. His last words, a disjointed, sleepy murmur, had been that she smelled sweet and clean...and that she wasn't to disappear, even if she was just a figment of a fevered imagination.

So Helen had stayed, lying locked in his sleeping arms, finding peace herself in the knowledge that she was needed. Perhaps she hadn't achieved the evening's reckless goal, but she had gained something infinitely more precious: a proud man's trust...a proud and *courageous* man, however cowardly he claimed to be...

At some point in her vigil she, too, fell asleep, and when she became conscious again it was to be aware that the man who had earlier come apart in her arms was no longer helpless...he was a man again. The hips that had sexlessly cuddled hers were moving in slow, sensuous circles that had parted her sleepy thighs, and a warm, caressing hand had tugged down the stretch lace of her bra so that her bare breasts spilled over the top into a warm cup of masculine fingers that gentled them to tingling life.

She had opened her eyes slowly, half afraid of what she would see in his face. Did he regret and resent that she had been witness to his breakdown? When she finally brought herself to look at him fully, her shock was instantly followed by a blush that mantled her entire body. Gone was the savage, hard-edged stranger, and in his place a lazy-eyed man whose smile was like a physical caress. His face still showed the bruised effects of exhaustion, but the tight, mask-like lines of strain had gone. At some stage he had shrugged out of his crumpled jacket and discarded his black tie, unbuttoning his white shirt to his flat waist. His body had the lean, tense hardness of an over-worked racehorse, sharp planes where there should be smooth ripples of flesh. She wanted to touch him, to discover what he felt like, the way he was discovering her, but her earlier reckless boldness had been short-circuited by events. Her fingers curled into her palms as she lay looking at him, wondering what he thought of her. The lamp arching over the top of the couch turned his hair to molten golden, and reflected sparks of amber into the dark brown eyes as he watched her sleepy wariness turn to shy confusion.

He laughed huskily. 'That's the first sleep I've had in six months that I haven't woken screaming from. Thank you.'

'For what?' she whispered, aware that with every breath the tips of her breasts brushed lightly against his bare chest, and that he was aware of it, too.

'For being here. For not turning away when I got ugly. For listening.' One finger lightly traced the navy shadows under her wide green eyes, where a faint crust of salt attested to her unwiped tears. 'For caring...'

'I ... We're not islands,' she murmured, fascinated by the difference in him, unknowingly aroused by it as much as by their physical proximity.

'I think I'd forgotten that.' His finger traced around her breasts to the catch of her bra, which he flicked open with skilful ease. His hands measured the incredible slenderness of her waist and the womanly bloom of her narrow hips, sliding around to cup her soft bottom and draw it more closely against his fullness, sighing as he absorbed the sensuous impact of her trembling response. 'I'd forgotten there was such a thing as innocence left in the world. Where I've just been, even the children are taught to be killers from the time they can carry a weapon, to admit no just cause but their own. I thought I was numb, dead inside, no feelings left, and that was the way I wanted it because where there's no feeling there's no pain. I didn't give a damn at that party, but you did ... you hurt me with a look ... you made me feel something and I wanted to hurt you for that ... and you let me. You would have let me do anything, because you were innocent, and innocence is its own in-built protection and strength. You were like a candle, placed in my hand to help me through the lonely night. So small, so fragile, but, oh ... such a lovely light ...'

'So you're a poet, too,' she managed to tease, feeling embarrassed by the intensity of his gratitude. She didn't want his thanks; she wanted, she wanted ...

'You inspire me,' he said, in a voice as silky-soft as the caress of his hands. 'You asked me to help you, and I said I couldn't. I was wrong. I've been wrong about so many things. I have a gift for you, I should be honoured if you would accept it ...'

How could she have forgotten such a gift? How could she have forgotten the sensual grace of his lovemaking? It hadn't been sex, not that first time, it had been too sweet and tender, bathing her entire body in such an exquisite spell of enchantment that she had cried for joy.

He had claimed that he had no gentleness...he was gentle to the point of pain, so delicate and slow in his prolonged seduction of her innocence that at last she had to turn aggressor, and teased him with her delightful wildness until he discarded that magnificent self-control and plunged with her into passionate turmoil. And after the gentleness he had shown her other paths to those Elysium fields: the rough and tumble, the playful, the fierce and intensely erotic, until they were both exhausted. But this was a sweet, healthy exhaustion, and when he slipped again into sleep, entwined with her on the big double bed in the blue and white bedroom, Helen had to resist the enticing temptation to do the same.

She didn't want to leave, but as dawn began to reveal the flaws in the jewel-encrusted city of lights outside the window, she knew she must. Reality ruled. She didn't want the awkwardness of farewells to ruin the memory of a magical night with a very special man. She had risen from his warm, relaxed body with sweet regret. Whoever he was, he had fulfilled her every desire, he had given her a memory that would always remain precious...

The irony of it. Now that she had remembered, how did she deny the specialness, the rightness of it, without sacrificing her self-respect? How could she banish it to its rightful place in her life when she wasn't sure where that was? No wonder she had reacted so strangely to seeing Alex... *again*. No wonder her body had been throwing out such strong hints. *It* had remembered even if she didn't...remembered that this man had once possessed her so totally that nothing else had existed...not his world or hers. He had built on his memory, used it, while hers had lain dormant until...until Greg...

'And this is where you'll do your piece, Greg...make those vows you wrote yourself, and then we'll do the traditional bit with the rings...'

The vicar's voice jerked Helen back to her surroundings, and she was grateful for the evening dimness of the church to hide her blushes. Was it a sin to think carnal thoughts in church? At your own wedding rehearsal? About another man? If only she could stop the mental pictures flickering through her head, but they had persisted with relentless constancy ever since Alex's departure from her flat the previous day.

Alex. It was impossible to think objectively about him any more, the illicit memories were too fresh, too new. In the space of a few weeks, he had turned her entire world upside-down. He didn't love her... he couldn't... not on the strength of one night and a few weeks' acquaintanceship. And how did she feel about this man, this intimate stranger? She didn't know. Everything had happened so fast, shock upon shock, that she didn't feel sure of anything anymore.

Even her feelings about Greg were all mixed up. Pray God that what she was preparing to do would clarify them for once and for all. At least she was in the right place to do that, she thought with a wry inward grin, although He would hardly give His blessing to a sin. But she had to know. Before she made her final vows to Greg she had to be certain in her heart that she could live up to them. She had to prove Alex wrong. She had to prove her love to *herself*...

Dear Greg. She watched him make a joking remark to the vicar. He was so good, so kind. She couldn't believe that he was still in love with a woman he hadn't seen for ten years. Perhaps he might have a special place in his heart for Alice, but that was understandable... just as Alex had created a little shrine to his 'Angel', who in reality had just been an innocent witness to his great moment of self-revelation. And now that she, too, had memories of a former lover to cope with, Helen could understand the reluctance to let go of them, especially if they were particularly... affecting. One could be a little 'in love' with the memory of someone without actually loving them in the *enduring* sense of the word.

That night, five years ago, she had set out to seduce a stranger, tonight she was going to seduce a friend. It was fitting that she and Greg were here rehearsing their wedding ceremony, for tonight, Helen had decided, they were going to rehearse their wedding night!

Greg didn't know it yet, but tonight she wasn't going to take no for an answer. She had only made her momentous decision after Alex had turned up at the shop that afternoon. Fortunately Helen had been helping out over at one of the other stalls and had seen the blond head, gleaming like a Viking invader's helmet in the midday sun, as he had ducked to enter her shop. She had made an excuse to the astonished stall-holder and fled, managing to fudge a believable reason for having some running around to do when she rang Nicola from the anonymous safety of a downtown cinema foyer. Alex had apparently searched the market for her, and then hung around talking to Nicola for over an hour before he had given up. Helen shuddered at the thought of her narrow escape. She couldn't have faced him, she couldn't! She sat through an entire movie without hearing a word of dialogue or seeing a frame of film, running her own personal picture show through her head, over and over, to try and lessen its impact. It hadn't worked. She couldn't hide from Alex for ever. For one thing, she had arranged weeks ago to stay overnight with Greg's parents after the rehearsal at the church, which was within walking distance of the Knights' home, and she couldn't think up a good reason to back out. Her lies and omissions had already stretched her creative imagination to its limits. Alexander Knight was doing a great job of turning her into a thoroughly deceitful hussy, she thought resentfully. She had cried off dinner before the rehearsal, but afterwards Hannah was going to give her the final fitting of her wedding dress, and Anna and Nicola their bridesmaid's dresses, also in the oriental style. Then Hannah and Helen were going to go over the catering arrangements. As the reception was being held at the house, the extended family were pitching in to help, and it was a matter of phoning with reminders and dealing with last-minute hitches.

When Greg had told her he, too, would be staying at the family home that night because the painters he had had in the day before had spilled a paint-thinner which had permeated the flat with an acrid stench that would take days to clear, the idea had emerged full-blown from the frantic recesses of her brain. It had become imperative that she wipe out the memory of herself in Alex's arms with a more stirring one: herself in Greg's arms. Only then could she face Alex with any semblance of serenity and confidence. Once before she had been driven into an impulsive action by the pressures of time; she only hoped that this occasion would prove as traumatic and . . . yes . . . enjoyable. It *had* to be.

As the small group filed out of the church, Helen suddenly realised that she hadn't absorbed anything that had gone on. She'd have to bone up on the service before Saturday! Nicholas, who had happily agreed to give her away, was strolling on ahead with Anna, while Doug Sellers, the best man, was making a move on Nicola, who was pretending to be coy. Helen took a deep breath and tucked her arm through Greg's, deliberately slowing him down so that they lagged out of earshot of the others.

'Greg . . .' her voice was husky with nerves . . . appropriately sexy, she thought '. . . I brought some of my going-away clothes with me tonight.' She was also going to stay at the Knights' before the wedding, so that, in Hannah's words, she could be 'pampered and cosseted on her last morning as a single woman' with the appropriate motherly devotion. Susan and Jack and the children were being put up there, too—the Knights' hospitality seemingly endless.

"Mmmm?" Greg was looking up at the clear black velvet sky. A single star was shining. What was he wishing for?

'Mmmm... I have this fabulous sheer lace nightgown that Susan sent me. Black French lace. I thought I might wear it tonight...'

Greg's steady pace faltered. Was his imagination supplying the details? She hoped so. Helen pressed herself a little closer.

'Why don't I model it for you?' she murmured invitingly.

'Helen...' Greg stopped. They were just outside the white picket fence which separated the footpath from the Knights' property. The gently stirring branches of the flowering cherries which lined the quiet suburban street hid the wishing star from their sight, but Helen hoped it was still working for her. 'Helen, are you suggesting what I *think* you're suggesting?' Greg asked in a startled whisper, even though the others were already on the doorstep.

Her answer was to link her arms around his neck and pull his mouth down to hers. At first restrained, his kiss soon became hard and hungry, almost desperate. Helen felt a quiver of apprehension which she firmly shrugged away. Whatever happened, there must be no regrets.

'Helen, I thought we'd agreed to wait,' Greg said shakily as they finally broke apart.

'Wait for what? I already feel married,' said Helen urgently. 'Please, Greg. I love you and I've already waited so long...'

'But tonight...in my mother's house...'

To her horror Helen found herself thinking that Alex wouldn't be so hard to seduce. He wouldn't care where he made love to her, all that would matter would be his pleasure . . . and hers.

'Greg, your parents are very heavy sleepers—it's a family joke—and anyway, they're not prudes, they have a very modern outlook.' More modern than yours, she wanted to say, but restrained herself. She wanted to make love, not start an argument. She leaned against his chest and tilted her head back provocatively. 'Don't you want me, Greg?'

For an awful minute he hesitated, then rushed into reassuring speech. 'Of course I do, darling. It's just . . . why tonight? Why not wait until we can use the flat?'

She ignored the questions she had no reasonable answer for, and traced his mouth with a firm finger. 'You've been away so much recently, I just need to feel close to you . . .'

'I want it to be perfect for you——'

'It will be,' she hoped fervently. 'Come on, Greg . . . where's your sense of fun and daring? We love each other, it's not as if we'd be doing anything so terribly wrong!' She waited impatiently for his reply, the adventurous spirit that had so attracted him to her burning brightly in her eager eyes. She was challenging him to make that final commitment, *now*.

'All right, if you're sure that's what you want,' he said warily, unwilling to dig any deeper into her sudden demand.

'You might sound a bit more enthusiastic about it!' she said tartly, and he grinned suddenly.

'I think I can manage to raise a modicum of interest.'

'I hope you raise *something*,' she grumbled wickedly, feeling the first major hurdle cleared. She waggled her eyebrows at him. 'Your place or mine?'

'I think it had better be yours,' he said, drawing her up the pathway. 'I promised to take Doug and Dad out for a few drinks while you girls are barricaded in the sewing-room. Besides, if I'm caught sneaking around in my bathrobe it won't be quite as compromising as you in your black French lace!'

Helen giggled nervously. 'I think we're already compromised, Greg. We're getting married on Saturday, remember? People would probably think it was suspicious if we *weren't* sneaking around with each other!' Her smile faded as she looked at his gentle, familiar grin. 'I *do* love you.'

If he thought her insistent emphasis odd, he didn't say so. 'I love you, too, Helen,' he said.

'Just don't come home drunk, or I'll be waiting with a rolling pin in my bed!' she mock-scolded as she opened the door.

'I'm driving, so there's no question of that, not with the drink-drive traffic blitz on...I don't want to find myself on the end of a *real* ball and chain at my bachelor party,' he joked as they both went into the bright warmth of the house.

A shadow detached itself from the open garage at the side of the house and moved into the soft glow of the porch.

Alexander Knight uttered a quiet, explicit curse into the clear, carrying night air.

So...his angel was running scared, right into the arms of the opposition. That had been a risk from the start, but one that he was no longer willing to entertain. Too much was at stake, for too many people.

Damn her for her loyalty and stubborn optimism...and love. All the qualities that he so admired in her were conspiring against him. He considered the very limited extent of his options. There was only one that appealed, for both supremely selfish and smugly altruistic reasons. Helen had no idea of the full consequences of her reckless actions. She was running blind. She needed to be saved from herself, much as she had saved Alex five years ago. She, too, needed to be shocked into facing the truth about herself...

Of course, she might very well hate him for the resultant humiliation, but at least she would be forced to stop and think, to pause in her headlong rush into the rosy glow of her imagined destiny.

Afterwards—well, he would cross that rather terrifying bridge when he came to it. He would trust to luck, and love. With a lot of both he might be able to catch a falling angel and keep it for his own. Possession, after all, is nine points of the law...

CHAPTER NINE

HELEN was humming as she bounced off the bottom stair and through the door into the kitchen.

'Morning, Hannah!' she carolled as the older woman greeted her with a smile.

Nicholas Knight, buried behind the morning paper at the head of the kitchen table, merely grunted and Helen raised her eyebrows. Nicholas was a notoriously cheerful riser, usually a mine of information about the weather prospects and the morning news and what he had managed to do in the garden while everyone else was sleeping away the best hours of the dawn. Hannah, carrying a cup of coffee across to place before her husband, gave Helen a wry grin. Had they had a marital spat? That, too, would be a departure from the norm. Helen had never known a more well-matched couple. Unless it was she and Greg! She beamed sunnily around the room...everything seemed brighter, sharper, more colourful this morning.

'You look full of beans,' Hannah said. 'I'm glad you had a good night. You've been looking a bit wilted lately.'

Helen sat down in a hurry, reached for the box of muesli, hoping her laugh would cover her sudden fluster. She imagined herself transparent with happiness, and was embarrassed that Hannah might guess the reason why. Could people tell? She tried to compress the heady bubbles that had expanded inside her brain, but they proved irrepressible.

It wasn't just happiness, but a general feeling of relief and well-being. She felt as if a great weight had been lifted off her heart. All her worries and doubts felled at one blow! Now she could look forward to her wedding with a clear conscience and an open heart.

She drank her juice and made dreamy inroads into her bowl of muesli, only half listening to Hannah's soft chatter. She felt lazy yet filled with boundless energy, tired yet elated. She didn't feel like going to work at all, but knew she ought to since she had several orders to clear up before the honeymoon.

Honeymoon. She sighed blissfully. She could almost wish that the fuss was all over, or that she and Greg could slink away to a register office and tumble straight back into bed and stay there. She grinned. What a scandal that would cause in the family ranks! She wished Greg would hurry up and come down. She wanted to see his face in the daylight. She wanted to see the mirror of her own joy in his eyes. She wanted to know if he felt as amazed and exhilarated as she did at the sheer volcanic force of last night's eruption. It had certainly taken her by surprise. Even though she had been fiercely determined to make it happen, she hadn't expected it to be so swift, so all encompassing, so... *easy*... She had thought she might have to work at conquering the memories, but instead they were quickly overwhelmed by reality.

It almost hadn't happened at all...

After Anna and Nicola had left and she had forced herself to concentrate on whether they should 'forget' to put out cousin Dorothy's execrable pasta salad and thus risk offence rather than food poisoning, and whether it was better to have a small quantity of good champagne or gallons of cheaper sparkling wine—they decided on the champagne, since Hannah's experience had taught her that most of the men would prefer beer anyway, and the women deserved a treat after all their cooking. After her bath she had spent ages preening in front of the mirror, wondering whether she should wear make-up, and was glad she hadn't, having forgotten that

Hannah usually came in with a cup of tea before re-
tiring. The men weren't back yet, she told Helen, not
turning a hair at the black nightgown. Considering that
Helen's normal bed attire when she slept over was un-
romantic pyjamas, she thought Hannah showed great
restraint. There was, however, a twinkle in her eyes when
she said her final goodnight that had Helen choking in
her tea.

She read for a while but she didn't think that the
bloodcurdling murder stories at hand were creating the
right mood, so she turned off the light and arranged
herself decoratively against the sheets and tried to think
sinful thoughts. Only that wasn't any good either because sinful thoughts inevitably led to Alex. Helen
punched the pillow and lay down again making her mind
a careful, peaceful blank. Several times she looked at
the luminous dial of her watch. Four hours? How long
did a 'few drinks' *take*, for goodness' sake? Surely Greg's
scruples weren't greater than his desire? No...he loved
her...of course he would come...he just didn't want
to make his father suspicious by making a big thing of
hurrying home!

Considering her state of anxiety and nervous tension,
it was a mystery how she managed to fall asleep, but the
next thing she knew she was being ruthlessly kissed by
a very naked male. A very *aroused* naked male.

'Greg...' At least she knew this one's *name*, she
thought semi-hysterically after her first hot flash of *dé
jà vu*. She put her arms up to brace against strong, warm
shoulders, and discovered that the bedclothes had already
been stripped away and her nightgown was similarly following suit. Lightly calloused hands slid up her thighs,
gathering the folds of the nightgown and raking it up
over her head in one deft, lifting movement. Helen was
flabbergasted. What was his hurry? This wasn't how she
had imagined it would be at all. She had thought they

would talk first . . . flirt and make verbal love . . . test the waters cautiously, together . . .

'Greg, wait——' she protested when she managed to free her mouth from his, gasping as he lowered his chest against her and she felt the burning heat of his skin firing her cool breasts. His heart was pounding violently in his chest, and she felt an answering thump of fear. He was so big and strong, the tension in his body barely under control. It wasn't the Greg she was used to at all. She had the feeling that she had unleashed a tiger instead of the gallant 'verray parfit gentil' Knight that she had expected as a lover. His full weight was now pressing her into the bed, his whisky-flavoured mouth hot and hard as it silked along her jaw and discovered the sensitive hollows of her throat. The light stubble on his cheek was like velvet sandpaper against the upper curve of her breasts, and the knot forming in her belly tightened. She felt trapped, overwhelmed, and she panicked. This was all wrong! She couldn't go through with it! She should have waited until after the wedding, when all the pressures were off. This wasn't the way to prove her love, she was *using* Greg and he deserved better than that . . .

'Greg, wait——' she repeated desperately, not altogether surprised when he ignored her. He'd had a few drinks—or maybe more than a few—and his normal inhibitions were loosened. He had been explicitly invited into her bed, and would have every reason to be furious with her if she now reneged. The only thing to do was to try to talk him down, to slow the situation down until he was prepared to listen, even though she didn't quite know what she was going to say. If only he hadn't woken her like that. For one, brief, shocking instant she had thought it was Alex, and his name had trembled on her lips, just as he had said it would. *No!* Perhaps if she could *see* Greg, look into his dear, familiar face, her attack of nerves would pass . . .

Helen threw out her arm, almost knocking over the bedside-lamp in her haste to find the switch.

'No.' Her arm was caught and pinned beside her head, the word a whispered growl as he reared up, his body arching so that the hardness of his hips burrowed into the softness of her thighs, impressing her anew with his enormous strength and power, except this time, instead of feeling a stab of fear, Helen felt another sensation, equally sharp and penetrating, streaking through her body. Her other hand was caught and pressed into the pillow on the other side of her head, and he tilted to one side, making a soft grunt as he hooked a foot around one of her ankles and thrust it outwards. She gasped as she felt the hot, velvety brush of his male hardness in intimate caress as he settled back on her spreadeagled body.

'But...I want to see,' she whispered, moving her head restlessly, flexing her wrists against his iron grip, no longer sure what she did want. Stop or go on? It appeared he wasn't allowing her a choice. Perhaps it was for the best.

'No. You don't have to see, just *feel*,' his rasping whisper was oddly thick, 'feel what you do to me...what I do to you.' He moved on her and she couldn't help but feel. Her toes curled as a tremor shot from the soles of her feet to the nape of her neck. 'You'll like it, love...such sweet blindness...'

His erotic words she heard through a strange roar in her ears, every nerve suddenly raw and exposed to each infinitesimal change in his body. In spite of the absence of light that made them both mere shadows on the narrow bed, she had never felt more vulnerable, more open, in her life.

He kissed her, lips and tongue ravishing her uncertain mouth until the hands he held captive began to help-lessly clench and relax in rhythm with the slow grind of his hips against her silky centre. His teasing thrusts went on and on until she couldn't bear it any longer, and she wrapped her legs around his to try and ease the ache he had created. He released her then, and her hands slid greedily over the slippery dampness of his shoulders and chest, finding the muscles knotted with cramping tension that echoed her own.

She was given no time to leisurely explore. Her touch sent him into explosive action, stroking, kneading, touching and tasting in a savage violation of her senses that aroused her most primitive instinct to bite and scratch and fight him for the pleasure of his possession. This was no tender seduction, it was a passionate mating that had Helen crying out for it to be over...for it to go on for ever...

'Ssshhh.' He covered her cries with his mouth. 'No noise, darling, not this time...If you want to scream, do it with your body, express it all in the way you move...'

'Greg——'

'Lover——' His hard mouth corrected her, his hands sliding beneath her to cup her arching bottom, preparing to make the appellation the literal truth at last. 'I'm your lover.' His husky whisper was as erotic as the strain of his hair-roughened thighs between hers. 'The only lover you'll ever need...ever want...'

'Yes, oh, yes...' she sobbed in sweet, passionate relief.

'Say it...my only lover.'

'My only lover——'

'Tell me you'll never love anyone else...'

'Never...anyone else,' she gasped, twisting in his implacable grasp. 'Only you...'

'No turning back.'

'I never want to go back. Oh, please...' There was no shame in begging, for he was begging, too, with his body. She could feel how close he was to an explosion, how his chest heaved and the arms braced beside her shoulders strained, as if he was a wild animal pulling against the leash. But his control held, by the barest thread, and he drew back at the last minute, rolling over and pulled her on top of him, lifting her so that he could find her swollen, aching breasts with his mouth, guiding her hands to the bedhead so that she could support herself while his hands were free to roam, urging her against the hard contraction of his belly as he brought her to the violent brink of ecstasy.

And then, with a single, powerful movement that stole the last of her shattered reason, he flipped her on to her back and came over and into her so hard and fast that her head spun, stretching her body into a taut bow beneath his as he wrenched her into paradise, cupping her head and pulling her face hard against his chest to muffle her helpless cries. When his moment came a split second later, she heard the grate of his teeth as he swallowed his harsh groans, his body relaxing with a final shudder into hers, married flesh to flesh by the dark . . .

'Helen?'

Helen blinked, a hot blush rising out of the open neck of her loose, short-sleeved blouse. Hannah was obviously expecting a reply, but Helen hadn't the least idea of the question.

'I said, would you like some more bacon and eggs?'

Helen looked down at her plate. To her utter astonishment she found she had devoured a meal she hadn't even been conscious of being served. Her ravenous thoughts had obviously been mirrored in her appetite.

'I'm quite happy to do you another egg. It's just that you don't usually like anything heavy before work.'

The newspaper at the end of the table rustled sharply and lowered a few inches. 'Oh, for goodness' sake, Hannah, stop nagging the girl.'

Helen's mouth dropped open. She had never heard Nicholas use that tone of voice on his wife before. Before his paper was hurriedly raised again she saw his eyes, and her mouth snapped shut. They were red-rimmed and bloodshot, the skin around them loose and pale.

She looked at Hannah, who nodded.

'Drunk as a lord,' she announced, and the paper snapped viciously. 'Got a head on him like an elephant, I shouldn't wonder. Another cup of coffee, dear?'

Nicholas folded the paper and looked blackly at his amused wife. 'You're enjoying this, aren't you?'

'It serves you right, dear. You should know by now that you always have to pay for overindulgence. Never could hold his drink,' she told Helen, who was trying hard not to giggle, relieved to have the spotlight off her own abstraction. 'That's why my parents encouraged me to go out with him. They knew he didn't drink like some lads, he was too afraid of making a fool of himself if he had more than a couple of shandies...'

'My capacity has expanded since then.' Nicholas seemed to think she had cast an aspersion on his manhood, and this time Helen did giggle.

'Mmmm, you certainly worked hard on it last night, apparently,' said Hannah serenely. 'He couldn't even make it up the stairs.' She winked at Helen, fuelling her giggles. 'Passed out on the couch. At least I was spared a night of drunken snoring. That also tends to be elephantine after a spree.'

'Looking a bit brittle around the edges, Dad.' Helen stiffened at the voice behind her. 'How about a little hair of the dog?'

Nicholas took one look at the tall glass of blood-red liquid set on the table before him, clapped a hand to his mouth, and sprinted for the back door.

'Alex, how could you?' His mother's voice trembled with laughter. 'You know your father can't stand bright colours on a morning after. He wouldn't even go down to the orchard for fear some of the plums were ripe.'

'Throwing up is the best thing for him, at this point. I guess I may as well have the Bloody Mary myself.' Alex sat down where his father had been, while his mother scolded and fetched the coffee.

Helen studied her own cup, conscious that Alex was staring at her. Now it came to the point, she was afraid to look at him. She had been very aware of him from the moment he had come into the room...*that* hadn't changed. But everything else had. She couldn't possibly have responded to Greg last night the way she did if her feelings for him had been superficial, and vice versa. They belonged together. That left Alex where he should have been all along...on the outside looking in.

'Good morning, Helen.'

She couldn't ignore him any longer. 'Good morning, Alex,' she said steadily, lifting her gaze until it collided with his. His elbows were on the table, chin resting on laced hands, his eyes as quiet as his voice, dark and grave and wary.

'Sleep well?' he murmured, and she felt herself begin to blush again. Did he know? Had he heard Greg sneak into her room? Had he, God forbid, heard the sounds that had escaped her? Her blush intensified until she was sure her guilt was written in letters of fire across her brow.

'Yes, thank you,' she said stiffly, pride coming to her rescue. She had done nothing wrong...only expressed her love for the only man in her life. And it wasn't a lie. She had fallen into a deep, satiated sleep in her lover's strong arms, cherished by the relaxed warmth of his body. When she had woken alone, she had felt more lonely than she had before in her life, even in the most despairing days of her illness. She wanted to wake in his arms as she had slept: safe, secure in his love. Where was he? Why didn't he come, so that she could see her knowledge mirrored in his beloved face?

'So did I.' He was making her feel uneasy again. He had lost that tense, restless look that he usually carried with him, even when he appeared relaxed. He smiled gently at her, and she was horrified to feel the warmth of it like a physical touch. She *couldn't* feel anything, not after last night, not unless she was a closet nymphomaniac! She jerked her gaze towards Hannah's comforting ordinariness.

'Where's Greg? Doesn't he have to be leaving for work soon, too?'

'Oh, I doubt that he'll be going *anywhere*.' Hannah's mouth quirked into an exasperated line as she poured a coffee for Alex. 'He's in a worse condition than his father. Didn't you hear them come in last night, Helen, singing and carousing? Greg apparently passed out on the floor in the lounge and he's still there...couldn't even stagger through to the other couch in the study. I washed my hands of the lot of them, and *you* can stop looking so angelic, Alex. When you offered to go along to do the driving so that Greg could enjoy himself, I thought you were planning to do him a favour, not get him legless. Nicholas told me all about the magnums of champagne you kept ordering for everyone in the bar while you sat smugly on a couple of whiskys all night. It really was too bad of you...I thought the driver in a drinking school was supposed to be the *restraining* influence...'

The black tingling which had begun to fizzle up Helen's spine when Hannah began her mock-severe lecture suddenly exploded into fully fledged horror. Greg had *passed out*? Blood coagulated in her veins, slowing her thought processes to a standstill. *Alex* had been drinking whisky? *Alex*?

Helen wasn't aware of standing up, until she had to grab the edge of the table for support. Her legs felt like rubber, her head buzzing, red dots dancing in front of her eyes. She looked at Alex and saw in his gravity quiet triumph, in his wariness guilt. Full realisation crashed down on her.

'*You!*' Her horrified whisper issued from bloodless lips. 'Last night. It was *you*!'

He leaned back in his chair, and the soft collar of his shirt shifted with the movement as Helen saw, on the side of his throat, a small red mark, like a burning brand... *her* brand. As she stared with blank, hypnotised eyes at the evidence of his monstrous deceit, he lifted his hand and ran a thumb lightly over the reddened skin. He showed no shame, no remorse for the terrible thing he had done to her.

'*My only lover*', she had called him, and it had been the literal truth. How he must have been laughing in the darkness, congratulating himself on his cleverness! She felt sick.

'What kind of man are you?' she whispered numbly, still not wanting to believe the evidence of her eyes. 'How could you *do* such a thing?'

'As it happened, a great deal more easily than I expected,' he said truthfully, and the blood which had drained from her face exploded back up under her skin, turning her scarlet with rage and shame.

'You utter bastard, Alexander Knight!' she screamed at him at the top of her voice. 'I wish to God I'd never set eyes on you. I hope you rot in eternal hell for what you've done!' And she burst into helpless, humiliating tears and rushed out of the kitchen, leaving Alex lunging to his feet, his mother exclaiming in shocked concern.

Blindly Helen stumbled through the first door she came to, seeking escape, a place to hide and lick her bleeding wounds. She almost fell over an untidy heap on the floor. Through the blur of her tears she saw Greg roll heavily on to his back, mumbling thickly, his eyes slowly cranking open to look at her standing over him.

'Helen, is that you?' He groaned. 'What happened? What's all the thumping?'

Helen had to bite her tongue to stop herself screaming at him too. She wanted to kick and shake him out of his drunken stupor, to blame him for what happened so that she wouldn't have to accept her own share.

With a moan she stepped over him and wrenched open the french doors, fleeing out into the summery freshness of the morning, taking in great gulps of sweet air to try and bring herself under control.

Alex. No wonder he hadn't wanted the light turned on. No wonder he had been in such a hurry to whip her into a sexual frenzy! He had been afraid that if she was in full command of her senses she would realise something was wrong... discover, even in the dark, the subtle discrepancies... the longer hair-length, the harder musculature, the odd timbre of his voice. But she hadn't... had she? Helen's headlong rush faltered, and she steadied herself against the solid out-thrown limb of an apple tree. One moment she had been thinking *I don't love this man enough*, the next she had been going up in flames... what subliminal signal had turned resistance to eagerness in the space of a few seconds?

'Helen?'

She turned so suddenly that she banged her head on the branch she had anchored to and saw stars... one bright, golden one in particular. As Alex reached automatically to help her, she remembered the last time he had assisted her, on the creek bank. With Alex, the cure was definitely worse than the illness! More infuriating still was the knowledge that she had been expecting him.

'Don't you touch me, you... you *animal*!' she spat at him, her eyes glittering like broken glass.

'Lucky for me you're an animal lover.' Alex grinned and Helen grew several inches in her outrage, tears vanishing along with her self-pitying weakness.

'You think it's a joke?' she roared at him, in a surprisingly big voice for a small woman. 'You think rape is something to laugh about?'

'It wasn't rape.' Concise. Succinct. True.

'I thought you were Greg,' she gritted at him.

'For the first five minutes, maybe,' Alex agreed, his tigerish smile distracting her from the grim purposefulness in his eyes. 'You wanted Greg to "wait". Me you begged to make love to you.'

'I didn't... I didn't even know it was you. It was dark——' It sounded feeble, even to her own ears.

'You'd know me if I was painted pitch black in a coalmine. It's called instinctive response, angel. You knew... but you wouldn't let yourself admit it because then you'd have to stop me... and you didn't want the loving to stop. It was a perfect marriage of ignorance and bliss. Speaking of which, how can you even consider marrying a man whom you have to bully into your bed?'

'I don't know what you're talking about.'

'What a shocking liar you are, darling. I was there in the front garden last night. I heard you putting the hard word on poor old Greg. I got the impression that it wasn't so much good old-fashioned lust on your side, as desperation. Maybe it unnerved Greg, too, because he was almost grateful for my efforts to get him blind drunk, and obliged with far more enthusiasm than he showed for your lemming-like seduction act.'

'Why, you——'

'Desperate situations call for desperate measures. I couldn't let you do it, Helen, not until I knew what prompted your sudden need to prove how much you wanted a man who doesn't really turn you on. All I intended to do when I came along to your room was find out, but then you grabbed me and I lost my head.'

'That's a damned lie,' Helen gasped. 'You didn't have any clothes on——'

'Actually I was still fully dressed, but when I touched your shoulder you turned over and put your cheek against my hand and murmured my name.'

'Liar!' said Helen hotly, all too afraid that it was true.

'And then you kicked your sheet off and I could feel that whisper-soft bit of nothing that you were wearing, and all my good intentions went for nought.'

'Good intentions?' Helen howled. 'You swine! You unprincipled lecher! You took advantage of me——'

'I hardly call it taking advantage when the lady is on top,' said Alex wickedly. As Helen's eyes closed in mortified remembrance, he took pity on her and said gently, 'I really did lose my head, Helen. You were lying there all soft and warm, dreaming restless dreams of me...I wanted to be in them with you, in *you*. All that repressed sexuality welling up inside me. I hadn't had a woman in five years, and suddenly, all my fantasies realised—you and I, together again. All the memories overwhelmed me...can't you understand how potent an aphrodisiac the mind can be?'

The morning light was harsh and revealing, and his eyes were hungrily devouring her every expression. Her very blankness gave her away.

Her eyes flew open as he drew a short, sharp breath between his teeth. 'My *God*!' he said in a shattered breath. 'You've remembered! *That's* what sent you into a panic. You've remembered everything, haven't you? And you didn't want Greg so much as you wanted to get rid of me.' His laugh was tight, hard, exultant as he watched her slow, painful blush. 'Don't you know, you silly girl, that you could spend the rest of your life going from bed to bed looking to find what we had...and never succeed? It's once-in-a-lifetime stuff!'

That was what she was very much afraid of. 'You egotistical——'

'Oh, cut the outrage, angel,' he said impatiently. 'I said *we*. If it wasn't mutual, it wouldn't be so spectacularly good. But how and when did it come back to you?' He didn't wait for an answer, his quick intelligence already working it out. 'Was it at the shower? Did I rewire some sensual pathways?' He laughed again, this

time with undisguised triumph. 'You can't escape your
destiny now, Helen, not after last night. You can't claim
the past doesn't matter.' His voice became soft and
lyrical. 'Come away with me, Helen, come see the world
with me. Or, better still, marry *me* on Saturday instead
of Greg. All the arrangements are made. All it would
take is a switch of grooms...'

His joke was the last straw. And if it wasn't a joke it
was the height of callousness.

'You really don't have much of an opinion of me,
Alex, if you imagine that I could dump Greg practically
at the altar and run off with someone else,' she said
shakily, shivering in her thin dress, even though the
morning was already hot and humid. 'Especially with
you. How can you even *suggest* such a thing? Unless
maybe it's what you've intended to happen all along.'

'You don't seem to have much of an opinion of me,
either, if you can believe that. I won't deny I'm a bit of
an opportunist...as a journalist it was a necessary asset,
and I won't deny that I've done my damnedest to stop
this marriage, but for your sake, not because of Greg.
I love you, Helen, and I think you love me. Are you
going to walk away from that? *Can* you? Are you going
to martyr yourself to guilt, the way that Greg has...and
cause a lot of needless misery in the process?'

She didn't know what he was talking about. Her head
throbbed and her limbs felt hot and heavy, and the
crushing weight of responsibility was back on her
shoulders. She couldn't marry Greg, but she couldn't
just walk out on him, *abandon* him, not after all that
they had shared. Falling in love with someone else...well,
Greg might be able to understand that from his own
painful experience, but falling in love with *Alex*? He
would never believe that his brother hadn't set out to
deliberately seduce her. This time the break between them
would be irreparable. Perhaps, in time...but no...Alex
wouldn't accept that. She could feel the force of his will

backing her up against the bough, pressing on her...demanding. If she broke off with Greg, Alex would immediately step into the breach. There would be no lies, no pretence about him. And Greg would know... Everyone would know and they would look on her with contempt and Alex with disgust. And Mr and Mrs Knight...they would be unbearably hurt, too.

'Helen, don't cry, we'll work it out.'

She hadn't even known that she was, but her hand came away from her face wet with despair and suddenly Hannah was there, firmly pushing Alex aside, ordering him back to the house.

'But—we need to talk,' he protested when his mother's plump figure blocked his move to reach Helen, now luxuriating in her tears.

'*You* may need to, but it's about time you considered what Helen needs. She looks at the end of her tether.'

'I...' For once Alex looked lost for words. He raked an impatient hand through his thick hair, and his mother's stern expression softened as she saw that the hand was trembling. 'You don't understand, Mum——'

'Oh, I think I understand more than you realise,' Hannah said, putting an arm around Helen's bowed shoulders. 'I'm not blind, Alex. But I think you've said and done quite enough for the moment. Poor Helen looks as if she's been bludgeoned over the head.'

'Mum——'

'It's all right, I won't ask what you did that was so awful. I do like to keep *some* of my illusions about your character, Alex.'

'I wasn't trying to hurt her.'

'Well, you apparently succeeded in spite of yourself,' his mother said with an asperity that made him wince. Through her glistening lashes Helen was fascinated to see him flush like an awkward little boy.

'Please, Mum, trust me.'

'I wouldn't dream of it,' said Hannah promptly, to Helen's inexpressible relief. 'You can be pretty merciless in your persistence, Alex, when you're on the trail of something you want, and I won't have you riding roughshod over the rest of us to get it. You know you'd regret it later, when it was too late. Now, go away or I'll call your father to come and deal with you.'

Alex was torn between frustrated anger and reluctant amusement. Amusement, and respect for his mother's judgement, won—barely. 'I doubt that Dad is capable of dealing with anything stronger than an aspirin at the moment, but I take your point. I'll go.' He backed off, his eyes on Helen's brittle face. 'But this isn't the end of it, Helen. When you finally stop behaving like a tragedy queen in a soap opera, you'll realise that everything's for the best.'

'Tragedy queen?' Satisfied that he had prodded Helen back into furious life, he turned and sauntered away. 'If your writing was as hackneyed as your *mind*, Alexander Knight, you'd get the Pulitzer Prize for Crassness!' she flung at his retreating gold crown and frowned blackly as his laughter floated back to them on the rustling breeze.

'He just wanted to get a rise out of you, dear,' Hannah voiced the conclusion that Helen had come to herself. 'I think Alex feels that any reaction is better than no reaction at all. Come over to the storage shed, Helen. There's something I think that you ought to see.'

With a final glare at the cause of all her problems, Helen followed the aproned figure around to the small, free-standing wooden building behind the garage. Already strands of hair were beginning to escape from Hannah's slipping bun, and Helen felt a lump rise in her throat as she wondered if she would ever see this warm and friendly woman again. Would Hannah ever forgive her for the embarrassment of a cancelled wedding? By cutting Greg out of her life, she would be cutting other ties which had been just as precious.

There was a single bulb hanging from the ceiling of the storage room, revealing walls of shelves crammed with articles of all shapes and sizes. Many of them were toys, and Helen ran her fingers over the faded paint of a big wooden tip-truck.

'That was Alex's,' said Hannah as she began shifting piles of books from one of the shelves. Helen snatched away her hand as if it had been scorched. 'Nicholas made that for him when he was four. It's funny, considering how active Alex was, you might have expected him to wear out his toys, but he was always very careful with his possessions. Not selfish, he was quite happy to let other children play with them, but he never took them for granted the way a lot of children do. We kept most of his toys. I always think it's lovely for grandchildren to be able to play with toys that were here when their parents were little. It gives them a feeling of continuity....'

'Which ones are Greg's?' Helen asked, to punish herself for gravitating to the truck.

'Ah, here we are.' Hannah ignored Helen's question as she pulled out a large cardboard carton, filled with loose photographs and old albums. She pulled up two dusty armchairs. Obviously, both she and Nicholas being dedicated hoarders, their fossicking was designed to be done in reasonable comfort.

'Now.' Hannah sat down and folded her plump hands over the album she had picked out of the box. 'You know, I look upon you as a daughter already, Helen. Now don't start looking guilty. As I said to Alex, I'm not blind. I do know that something's been troubling you the last few weeks. You're not quite the same happy girl you were when you got engaged.'

'Hannah——'

'Now, don't interrupt me when I'm on a roll,' said Hannah with a smile that was an echo of Alex's, and Helen subsided. 'I also realise that whatever doubts you have about you and Greg only arose after you met Alex.' Hannah sighed. 'I love both my sons, but they both seem to have a genius for getting in the way of each other's happiness. I, for one, am fed up with it. If you love Greg, marry him. If you don't, even if you're not sure, don't. It's as simple and as hard as that, Helen. You can't compromise. But I don't think that's the whole of your problem, is it?'

Helen shook her head before the maternal, all-seeing eyes.

'How much do you know, about what happened with Alice?'

Helen told her, falteringly, and Hannah nodded. 'I thought so.' She squared her shoulders beneath the flowered summer dress. 'I may be an interfering old woman, Helen, but I'd rather be thought that than un-caring. That's what Alex thought when his marriage broke up—that he'd get no support from us because we cared more for Greg and Alice, the wrong-doers, than we did for him. I've bitterly regretted my silence on that occasion. I hoped that my suspicions were unfounded, that it would all fizzle out and Alex need never be hurt. I felt if I interfered, both of them would hate me for it. Well, I learned my lesson. I'm not going to make the same mistake again.

'It was all the more painful because I liked Alice so very much. I still do. We keep in touch.' Hannah paused to let the shock sink in. 'I have some pictures here.'

Helen opened the proffered album gingerly. The wedding photograph caused a sick pang of jealousy. Alex looked so young, so carefree, and Alice...she looked just as vital, tall with nut-brown hair and eyes, strikingly beautiful. Helen hated her. She turned the pages, viewing the progress of a marriage, noting that there seemed far

more shots of Alice and Greg after the first few pages
than there were of Alice and Alex...and that the candid
shots of Alex captured perfectly his restlessness, his desire
to be somewhere else than frozen in the camera's eye.

'I think Alice knew, almost straight away, that she
had made a mistake, but she was a very conscientious
woman...she was determined to make the best of
it...until she fell for Greg. If she'd met him first, I don't
think that, exciting and excited as Alex was in those days,
there'd have been any contest. Alice came from a very
insecure background...her parents split up several times
when she was in her early teens...and she developed a
very thin veneer of sophistication to cope. I don't think
even *she* realised how much she wanted the security of
a traditional marriage rather than an absentee one,
however glamorous. I think she and Greg were kindred
spirits, he has a very traditional approach to marriage,
too. Their conservatism has been part of the problem.'

Has been? Not 'was'? Helen found herself staring at
the photograph on the page in front of her. Alice, a
mature Alice, her youthful beauty ripened into a warm
attractiveness and, tucked in the curve of her arm a boy,
about ten, tall and vulnerably thin. The shot was taken
too far away to see the colour of his eyes, but there was
a set to his skinny shoulders in the striped T-shirt, the
cocky slant of his hand hooked in the top of his jeans,
the proud lift of his head, that stopped the breath in her
throat.

'Who's that?' she croaked, pointing.

'That's Joshua,' said Hannah quietly. 'Alice's son.'

'Her son,' Helen repeated numbly. There was little of
Alice about him, he was a Knight from the top of his
wheat-gold hair to the soles of his sneakers. 'He never
told me,' she whispered achingly. 'He never told me he
had a son. Oh, God...' She was shattered by his lack
of honesty, his lack of *trust*. He spoke so glibly of love,
why had he been so silent about the love of his child...for

how could he not love his own flesh...even if he no longer loved the boy's mother?

'Who didn't tell you?'

'Why...Alex!' His name was an anguished cry of betrayal.

'It wasn't his place to tell you, Helen. Joshua isn't Alex's son.'

The album bumped unnoticed to the dusty floor, heat replacing the icy coldness in her face and hands as she realised both what she had just revealed to Hannah, and what Hannah had revealed to her. 'You mean...Joshua is *Greg's* son?'

Hannah nodded, bending to pick up the fallen album to give Helen time to recover her composure. 'Alice didn't find out until three months after she and Alex were separated, and she knew there was no question of the baby being his. She was in Australia with her parents by then, so she found it easy enough to keep her pregnancy a secret. We only found out after the birth, when she had a breakdown and her parents contacted us to get Greg's permission to take on guardianship of Joshua until Alice was well again.'

'Oh, Hannah!' Helen's own problems paled into insignificance. Thank goodness that her irresponsibility last night hadn't extended *that* far—she had ensured that she was protected. Alex's child...she could see him in her mind's eye, full of his father's golden splendour. Oh, no, Helen, don't get carried away by impossible dreams...

'Greg, of course, immediately blamed himself for her breakdown. At least it shook him out of the terrible apathy that had even lost him his job at the time. He flew straight over to see Joshua, and when Alice got better he wanted to marry her. But they both felt there were too many strikes against them. Her divorce from Alex wasn't through, and I think that as time passed their sense of shame increased, especially with Alex flinging himself into all sorts of danger. I shudder to think what would have happened if he had been killed. Alice and Greg would have felt even more responsible. So, since they didn't have the right to happiness together, they made other arrangements. They agreed visiting rights, and Greg sees Josh whenever he goes to Australia. Alice wrote me that she had never stopped loving Greg, but that she considered it a judgement on her sin that he could never look at her without remembering his guilt. I thought it was all rather overdone, but you know that for all Greg's placidity he can be quite as single-minded as Alex. And Alice had Joshua to occupy her. After Greg's business got going she accepted an increased maintenance for Josh—he goes to private school—but she was too proud to take anything for herself. She went back to writing, and ironically is actually enjoying it . . . perhaps she realises now that security comes from within, not without . . .'

'Hannah, why are you telling me all this?' asked Helen, interrupting the other woman's musing.

'Because Greg obviously hasn't told you. In spite of everything, I think that in the back of his mind Greg always thought that one day he and Alice and Joshua would be the proper family that they were meant to be. But time is getting on, and although Alice has never got serious about anyone else, she still insists that she could never forget the pain that she caused both Alex and Greg. So I think Greg decided that it was time to put the past behind him. I think he even means to sever the last bond with Alice by easing off his visits to Joshua. He loves that boy, Helen, but he believes that Josh needs a father who's there for him, all the time. Perhaps he feels that if he stays away Alice might find someone suitable. I have my doubts. And I think denying his own son will make him deeply unhappy. I have the feeling that, lately, he's come to realise that himself . . .

'I also believe that you have a right to know these things before you make an irrevocable decision about your future. You must do what *you* think is right, not what might be right for Greg...or for Alex.'

'But I don't know,' Helen wailed. 'I don't know what's right for me any more!'

'You don't think it might be Alex?' asked Hannah gravely.

'I don't know...' She no longer saw the point in prevaricating. 'He says he loves me but...I just don't know whether it's just the *circumstances* or something that's *real*...'

Tactfully Hannah didn't enquire of these mysterious 'circumstances'. 'It all boils down to you, then, doesn't it? How *you* feel. Whether you trust your own feelings for him...whether you believe him. He's a grown man, Helen, I should think he's mature enough to know his own mind.

'But if you're not sure, why don't you go away for a while and work it out? Why don't you call your sister and go and visit? You've always wanted to go to Hong Kong.'

It made a bizarre kind of sense...to go back to where it had all started.

'But...I can't just *go*. I mean...what about the wedding, my dress...all the presents...and the food——' Helen's voice began to rise alarmingly as she contemplated the chaos that would follow in the wake of her change of mind. 'All the invitations, the *family*...what will they all think?'

'You let me worry about that,' said Hannah calmly. 'It'll be a five-day wonder.'

'But Greg...he'll know it was something to do with Alex——' she panicked, leaping up from the lumpy armchair as if she expected her soon-to-be ex-fiancé to come raging out of the woodwork.

'So it is,' Hannah pointed out. 'Who knows, maybe this *is* for the best, as Alex says. Maybe this way Greg will feel that he's finally paid off his debt. Maybe he'll feel free to go after Alice with the same determination that he went after you. That's what Alice needs, you know, proof that Greg cares enough to *fight* for her love. And maybe that's what you're looking for from Alex.'

'You make it sound so simple and inevitable!' Helen sighed, feeling that she now knew where Alex got his serene self-confidence from. It must be an inherited trait!

'Perhaps it is,' smiled Hannah. 'You never know, all my work on that lovely dress might not be wasted, after all . . .'

CHAPTER TEN

IT WAS him.

Helen stared across the crowded courtyard to the man standing in the flare of the pool lights, her hand clenching involuntarily around her glass. He had his back to her but that blond hair brushing the collar of the light blue jacket was heart-rendingly familiar. Forgotten was the tiredness that had dogged the long days, the lingering jet lag that every so often slanted the world under her feet, reminding her that she was an alien in an alien land. Forgotten was her annoyance with Susan, who had insisted on dragging her along to the function organised by the huge apartment block's social club—an Australian wine and cheese evening held out by the Olympic-sized swimming pool. 'It'll cheer you up,' Susan had insisted callously; but it hadn't, it had merely made Helen more morose and aware how boring each and every man on the planet was... except the one she had left behind.

Beyond the swimming pool were the tennis and squash courts, and the children's playground where the mainly Filipino *amahs* took their charges every day to exercise their high spirits... all luxuries that Hong Kong expatriates took for granted when the husbands worked for multinationals like Jack's company. Dutifully doing the rounds of the markets, taking little Carolyn, Michael and Lisa to Ocean Park and Water World, Helen found her enjoyment of her more leisurely stay at the tiny Crown Colony tainted by anxiety. Had Hannah managed as easily as she'd claimed she would? Had Greg forgiven her? When he had finally sobered up enough to realise that she was calling off the wedding, he had been at first remorseful for standing her up, and then, when he'd discovered that she was in deadly earnest, accusing. Not being able to deny his suspicions had double-damned her in his eyes, and he had eventually stormed out in a fury, cursing her entire sex.

'He'll come round,' Hannah had soothed, seemingly unconcerned at being lumped in with her despicable sisters. It was Hannah who had made the phone call to Hong Kong and booked the one-way ticket on a flight leaving the next day, and it was Hannah who had kept a tigerish Alex at bay as he demanded to know what the hell was going on. He was persuaded to give Helen some breathing space, and she shuddered to know how he had reacted when he turned up at her apartment the next day to find her gone. She had half expected a furious phone call on her arrival, or even hot pursuit, but as the days passed she had forced herself to face the very real possibility that she could waste her whole life waiting for Alex.

He was gone. The blond man suddenly wasn't there any more, and Helen's heart stopped and then began to beat again, jerkily. Of course it wasn't him. She had to nip this obsession she was developing in the bud before it drove her crazy. Not every blond man was Alex. Alex was not every blond man. He was unique. And she had walked out on him, flat, without a word. Why should he bother to come after her? After all the things she had said to him, why should he think that she would welcome him? He was probably back in New York by now, starting on his new book. He was probably tucked away in his brownstone house, fielding calls from hordes of beautiful women eager to assuage any feelings of rejection he might have. Now that Alex's sexual fast had been broken, he might feel free to begin to live up to his reputation!

Oh, why had she been in such a hurry to escape the consequences of her actions? Alex probably despised her as a coward. And she had never told him that she loved him. Why hadn't she at least found the courage to explain that she wasn't afraid of loving him too little, but rather, too much? If only she had left him a letter. That would have been the *decent* thing to do. But then, Helen had behaved rather despicably all round. She shouldn't feel guilty about Greg, considering he hadn't behaved very well either, but she couldn't help worrying about him. If only she could have that time over again she would handle things very differently.

'Voulez-vous couchez avec moi ce soir?'

Helen dropped her claret. The glass smashed to tiny splinters on the smooth paving, red wine staining the expensive white Italian leather shoes she had been bullied into buying that morning by Susan.

'It sounds so much more romantic in French, don't you think?' Alexander Knight murmured, mopping at the tiny, blood-like spatters that had landed on his pale blue trousers with an inadequate blue silk square.

'Did you just say what I think you said?' Susan bristled at Helen's side.

Alex smiled down at Helen's pale, stunned face, thinking wryly that it had become a rather habitual expression when he was around . . . but not for much longer. 'I asked the lady if she would like to sleep with me.'

Susan, when her protective big-sister instincts were aroused, could be savage, but somehow this tall, handsome man in his fashionable new—they had Hong Kong written all over them—clothes took the edge off her anger. Helen was staring at him wide-eyed, the first sign of interest she had shown in anyone or anything all week. She'd even ridden the Dragon roller-coaster at Ocean Park the previous weekend without turning a hair. Helen—who hated thrill rides. That was when Susan really began to be concerned about her sister's state of mind . . . or lack of it.

'Well, the lady isn't interested,' said Susan firmly, drawing Helen away from where the Number Four Australian red was being swept up along with the glass splinters by one of the staff who helped keep the communal parts of the huge apartment complex scrupulously clean. 'She's suffering from a broken heart, and the last thing she needs is some macho stud stringing her a line.'

'Are you? Suffering from a broken heart?' The dark, well-remembered eyes reflected the shifting lights of the evening.

Helen nodded dumbly, her hand against her breast. Her heart was certainly beating fit to burst!

'You should get some expert advice. They're very dangerous things, broken hearts, especially if you try and mess with them yourself.' The curve of his mouth was subtle and sensual, his voice as smooth and voluptuous as the claret had been. 'I'm very good at mending hearts.'

'In bed?' Helen asked huskily.

'Helen!' Susan had been right to worry. Helen had finally flipped her lid. 'Are you a resident here, sir? Do you have an invitation?'

'In bed, out of bed, everywhere...wherever you want.'

'Look, buster, if you don't back off I'm going to call Security——'

'I have a suite at the Hilton.' Alex fumbled in his jacket pocket, not taking his hungry gaze off her face. Helen was sure he could see her answering hunger, and her heart, in her eyes. 'This is my room key. If you need a while to think about it...I don't want to rush you. I'll be waiting, for ever if necessary.'

'What in the hell is going on here?' Susan demanded angrily as he pressed the key into Helen's hand. Helen looked at it. It symbolised so much. The key to his life. The key to love. The key to freedom from the prison of her own uncertainty.

'Does my sister *look* like the kind of woman who would fall into bed with a total stranger? Where's Jack? He'll soon settle your hash!'

'I don't have to think about it,' said Helen softly. 'Of course I'll come.' She handed the key back to him.

'Helen!'

'I don't want to lure you back with me under false pretences. I do want a little more than just to make love to you day and night for the rest of my life.'

'Oh?' Helen quavered, conscious that they were playing a delicious game, with each other and with poor distracted Susan. How could she ever have doubted he loved her? She was disgusted at her own lack of faith.

'Helen!' The warning was hissed in her ear. 'Don't, for goodness' sake, encourage him. The man is obviously a kink!'

'You have to marry me.'

'Of course I do.' And she smiled at him for the first time, her eyes full of wicked innocence. 'After seducing you, the least I can do is make an honest man of you.'

'Helen, do you *know* this man?' Susan asked dangerously.

Alex grinned. 'She got there, finally. You must be Susan.' He took her limp hand and shook it. 'I'm Alexander Knight.'

'Alex?' Susan looked from one to the other. '*Your* Alex?' she asked Helen. 'The one who——?'

'The very same,' confirmed Alex, rather glad that Helen had had someone of her own to confide in.

'You took your time about it,' Susan announced baldly. 'Why weren't you on the next plane?'

'I had some things to do first,' said Alex mildly.

Helen stiffened. 'Greg?'

The dark eyes narrowed. 'Does it make a difference? Do you need his permission?' Helen shook her head without even having to think, and he sighed. 'I thought he might come after me, but he didn't. He settled for making Mum and Dad's life a misery for a few days, being a martyr over all the cancelled arrangements——'

'I knew I should have stayed,' whispered Helen guiltily.

'You were well out of it, darling,' Alex told her. 'I helped, too...with some relish, I might add. Greg left for Australia yesterday…ostensibly to visit Josh. Perhaps he and Alice will be able to work something out, after all.'

'Will you mind?'

His look asked whether she was crazy. 'The whole world can go to hell as long as I have you. God, I've missed you!' He put his arms around her and hugged her close, rubbing his cheek against her raven hair, loving the feel of her. She hugged him back and he groaned. 'Do you know what hell you've put me through these last few weeks? Well, now it's time to do your saviour act again. If only the Hilton weren't so far away!' He groaned again.

A jingle broke them out of their mutual absorption. Susan was dangling a bunch of keys, a wry look of amusement on her face. 'Why wait? There's an apartment upstairs and a big double bed in the spare room. Jack and I won't be up for at *least* another hour, and I doubt the children will wake unless you're *very* noisy…'

Two hours later, dewy-skinned and languorously happy, Helen watched Alex, wrapped in a white robe of Jack's, slide open the balcony door from the bedroom and step out into the warm night.

'Good God!' he exclaimed, and Helen somehow knew he wasn't referring to the view from the fourteenth floor. He was staring intently at something across the road from the towering stack of apartments. 'Is that what I think it is?'

Snagging the sheet off the bed, Helen swathed it around herself and joined him, hugging his long, lean back, her hands crossed at his waist. 'The American Club,' she confirmed, peeping around him at the floodlit peach building which possessed the only stretch of genuine lawn she had yet been privileged to see in Hong Kong. 'Rather a horrible coincidence, I thought, that Susan and Jack should choose to live right across the street. I couldn't escape the memories of you if I'd *wanted* to.'

Alex turned and leaned against the glass half-wall that rimmed the balcony, kissing her with slow pleasure. 'But you didn't want to escape them, did you?'

'I love you. I was afraid it might all have been a lovely illusion.'

'Then you can imagine how I felt when you denied even knowing me. I'd come from New York, prepared to be magnanimous and make sure you were happy——'

'Really?' Helen teased.

'Well, I will admit to a certain ambivalence. I wanted you to be happy, but as soon as I saw you again I knew I wanted you to be happy with *me*. I knew how Greg felt about Alice and Josh, and I couldn't bear the idea of you having the leavings. Discovering you didn't even remember me was merely a setback. You were loving and loyal, and quite justifiably suspicious of my motives, but I never lost hope because a woman deeply in love with one man doesn't respond to another the way that you did with me...only with me.'

'Why didn't you tell me about Josh?' she asked the question that had been nagging her all week. 'You must have known that it would have been the last straw...his not having told me...'

He cupped her jaw, his gentleness bringing tears to her eyes after the fierce passion of a little while ago. He loved her in all ways, in all of his moods. She was real to him, not just a dream.

'I cared what you thought of me. I wanted your respect as well as your love. You already thought I was an unprincipled swine for tricking you into making love with me, I had to prove I had *some* honour left. Besides,' his gravity side-slipped into a grin, 'I knew by then that you weren't going to marry him. All I had to do was sit back and wait. If I'd known you were going to run out on me I would have chained you to my side and betrayed my soul to keep you there.'

'Liar.' Helen didn't believe him. 'You knew I needed this time away. You knew I'd find out I was miserable without you——'

'Actually, I couldn't get a flight. It's a very popular time of year to visit Hong Kong. I had to bribe a booking clerk to bump me up the wait-list to get here this soon.'

'Alex!' She didn't know whether she was being teased or not, but it didn't matter. He was here, that was all that mattered now.

'I was only notified at the last minute . . . I didn't even have time to pack a toothbrush . . . but I *did* have time to shop after I got here . . . while plucking up the courage to find out whether my autobiography would have a happy ending . . . that's my next project, by the way.'

He pushed her back inside the room and made her take off the sheet and sit naked on the bed while he produced a small black box from his jacket, which lay crumpled on the floor. He took off his robe and sat on the bed beside her as he opened the box and took out a ring, a thin, gold circlet set with a line of yellow diamonds.

'Why do we have to be naked? Is this some kinky ceremony?'

'I like to be naked with you. Now, be serious.' He rearranged his lecherous expression into gravity as he placed the ring on her finger. 'With this ring, I thee wed. No engagements for us, Mrs Knight—you don't have a very good track record. Until we can do it legally, you can consider this binding.' He kissed her and they fell back on the bed, Helen admiring the ring over his shoulder and giggling when he ordered her to concentrate.

'It's beautiful, Alex, thank you.' She flashed it experimentally. 'It looks just like a halo of light.'

'Mmmm.' Alex was doing some experimenting of his own. 'And it fits perfectly!'